A LONELY PLACE TO DIE

'The old lady — with a bustle.' These words, uttered by Vincent Stroud before he was murdered, set Peter Gayleigh once again on the adventure trail. He becomes interested in a remote castle in Scotland where something very odd appears to be going on. His determination to solve this mystery brings him into contact with Shirley Quentin whose father, the owner of the castle, has disappeared. Finally, on a Scottish moor, Gayleigh meets the Herr Doktor Ulrich von Shroeder, a biochemist and master spy.

COLIN ROBERTSON

A LONELY PLACE TO DIE

Complete and Unabridged

LINFORD
Leicester

First published in Great Britain by
Robert Hale Limited, London

First Linford Edition
published 2005
by arrangement with
Robert Hale Limited, London

British Library CIP Data

Robertson, Colin, 1906 –
    A lonely place to die.—Large print ed.—
Linford mystery library
    1. Gayleigh, Peter (Fictitious character)—Fiction
    2. Scotland—Fiction
    3. Detective and mystery stories
    4. Large type books
    I. Title
    823.9'14 [F]

    ISBN 1–84395–895–3

Published by
F. A. Thorpe (Publishing)
Anstey, Leicestershire

Set by Words & Graphics Ltd.
Anstey, Leicestershire
Printed and bound in Great Britain by
T. J. International Ltd., Padstow, Cornwall

This book is printed on acid-free paper

Prologue

The old lady — with a bustle.

The words flashed through Stroud's mind again as he closed the front door behind him, his keen gaze travelling over the front garden. It presented a contrast in light and shade, a host of lurking shadows that stimulated his imagination, though for the time being the danger was past, he told himself.

During the long drive home he had cursed the clear night and the full moon. It had illuminated the road, seemingly with malific glee. But now he had reached the temporary safety of his house in Maida Vale, where he had garaged his car before seeking the warmth and comfort of the room he had just left.

Even then he had known he couldn't afford to relax. He must phone Shirley . . .

When he had stopped on the A1 to phone his wife, Ethel, to let her know he would be home shortly, he had little

1

realised that he would soon be driving for his life. For only minutes after making the call he had seen the other car — following him.

The pursuit had begun.

During that frantic chase south they had even attempted to halt him with bullets on a deserted stretch of the road. Then he had overtaken a police car which had been his salvation. He had not sought official assistance, but had kept behind it, and with the aid of his unwitting escort had reached London. The pursuit had been abandoned.

The old lady — with a bustle . . . The old lady — with a bustle . . .

Yes, he must contact Shirley at once. Not from his house. There was a call-box just along the road.

He set off briskly towards it, his thoughts reverting to Ethel. Of late her curiosity had developed into suspicion. Hardly surprising, of course, since he had been unable to explain his frequent absences from home. Usually, it had not been for very long, after office hours, but on this occasion he had been away several days.

'Vincent! Where *have* you been?'

She had asked him again that night, and as before his reply had been deplorably inadequate.

'Sorry, dear. Just business.'

In the early days he had given her fictitious details, but now she didn't ask for them, her cold acceptance of his comings and goings due to growing bitterness. He knew that, just as he knew there was nothing he could do about it. Nothing. Quite evidently she thought there was another woman. There was — but he was not involved in the way she imagined.

'I've — er — left something in the car. Shan't be more than a few minutes,' he had told her that night.

The old lady — with a bustle.

There had been a time when he had smiled at the fanciful imagery inherent in the phrase. It had amused him. But not now. It was pregnant with danger.

Footsteps!

He halted abruptly in the deserted street. The distant sound grew into a measured tread. Fully half a minute passed before a burly figure emerged from a side turning and began to approach. Only a constable on the beat. A symbol of security.

He reached the telephone-box and was stepping inside when the uniformed figure paused only a few feet away. He eyed the younger man with interest, and Stroud felt constrained to utter a perfunctory greeting.

'Good night, officer.'

'Good night, my friend.'

The guttural enunciation together with the cynical tone of the response halted Stroud, a surge of ghastly premonition coursing through him. Then he saw the Luger pistol, fitted with a silencer that suddenly appeared in the man's hand.

There was a sharp *plop* — and Vincent Stroud lurched backwards, a bullet hole in his temple.

His murderer caught him as he fell, supporting the limp body. He stepped into the telephone-box, closed the door. A few moments later a saloon car appeared from the side street, came towards him, and slid quietly to the kerb . . .

Part One

1

1

Peter Gayleigh returned to his flat in Jermyn Street to find Herrington waiting for him in the lounge. The Chief-Superintendent was settled comfortably in the gathering dusk, a glass of whisky at his elbow.

'Hullo, Peter!' He nodded towards his glass. 'I took the liberty of helping myself. After the somewhat chilly reception I got from your man, I felt I could do with it.'

'Carver has the right idea,' Gayleigh told him sardonically, as he mixed himself a drink. 'At various times quite a few policemen have called here with search warrants and very unkind ideas.'

'I know,' Herrington said dryly. 'We all admit you're smart.'

'But generous enough to assist you on occasions.'

'Well — yes.' Herrington looked at him

dubiously — a look prompted by a long vista of memories, for he had crossed swords with this debonair adventurer many times in the past, though now a brittle friendship existed between them. 'All right, let's cut the patter. You know why I'm here. What have you got for me?'

Peter lit a cigarette, inhaling deeply, the sardonic gleam fading from the steel blue eyes.

'I can answer that in one word — nothing.' He took a photograph from his breast pocket, that of a man about 35 with a rather studious face. 'I have hawked this through the highways and byways of Soho. I have shown it to all my low friends, my contacts I believe you call them. I have been in clubs, dives, and cafés. In short, I have displayed all the pertinacity of the paid sleuth. But nobody could identify this man. Apparently nobody had ever seen him.'

'H'm.' Herrington pursed his lips. 'Well, that's that. A pity.'

He was getting to his feet when Gayleigh pushed him very firmly back into the armchair.

'Oh no! Just a minute, Herrington. If it isn't asking too much I'd like to know a little more about this man. Yesterday, you will recall, you came here complimenting me on my unrivalled knowledge of Soho, asked for my help, and thrust this photo into my hand. Since then I've been giving a first rate impersonation of an unofficial and unpaid liaison officer between the police and what is melodramatically termed the Underworld. Now, I think, I'm entitled to know what's going on.'

It was not the first time Herrington had sought his assistance, and in his more righteous moments Peter Gayleigh marvelled at the unique position he enjoyed. That an adventurer who lived by his wits, cocking a mocking finger at the law, should have earned the grudging respect and, to some extent, even the confidence of the police, was, he felt, no mean achievement. For it had not always been so. It had taken some time for the elegant or, as he had been termed, the dangerous Mr. Gayleigh to prove both his quality and his eel-like propensity for wriggling out of difficult situations.

He flicked the photograph with his fingernail.

'Your move, Herrington.'

Herrington said: 'Does the name 'Shirley' convey anything to you?'

'No, I can't say it does. But perhaps if you could give me time to delve back into my misspent youth — '

'Don't trouble,' dryly. 'I've a hunch this girl picks her friends very carefully.'

Peter chuckled. 'Perhaps the surname might help.'

'It's Quentin — Shirley Quentin.'

'H'm . . . ' His brow wrinkled in thought. It suggested an intense effort of recollection but, in fact, was not. For the name had registered immediately. He recalled the salient facts of an engagement announcement he had read in the newspapers nearly a year ago: ' . . . Alan Sinclair, London, to Shirley Quentin, daughter of Stewart M. Quentin, D.Sc, Scotland.'

He had known Alan Sinclair at Cambridge. They had corresponded at infrequent intervals ever since, and Gayleigh had seen him occasionally in town, so he had never quite lost touch with him. But now he stared at Herrington blankly, feeling an irresistible urge to investigate this matter further on his own account.

'Shirley Quentin,' he echoed, shaking his head. 'No, never heard of her.'

Herrington sighed. 'A great pity. I thought you might have done. Now see if you can solve this one — the meaning of a certain phrase.'

'All right, I'll play. Let's have it.'

'The old lady with a bustle.'

Peter stared at him suspiciously. 'I'd hate to think you're pulling my leg.'

'No, I'm quite serious.'

'Indeed!' He flicked the photograph again. 'I'm not interested in old ladies. I'm interested in this man. I've a feeling you already know who he is.'

Herrington didn't deny it. He lowered his head, feeding tobacco into the charred bowl of his pipe.

'Very well, I'll tell you,' he said presently. 'The body of the man was found in a cellar, under the floorboards of an empty house. It had been empty for years and the body was in an advanced state of decomposition. It was only found when the house was being demolished, together with others in the vicinity to make way for rebuilding. According to the Home Office pathologist the man had been dead for at least nine months. He had been shot through the head.'

He paused to light his pipe, looking at Gayleigh over the darting flame of the match.

'Actually, I'm not surprised you drew a blank in Soho. He doesn't appear to have been the type of man who'd frequent that quarter.'

He broke off again, eyeing the glowing tobacco as if to satisfy himself that it was burning evenly. But the pause was deliberate, made with the sole intention of fanning Gayleigh's curiosity.

'Well, go on. What type of man was he?'

Herrington shrugged. 'Very respectable, it seems. He was a civil servant. His name was Vincent Stroud.'

The name meant nothing to Peter. He had never heard it before, though it was to provide the fuse which set him blazing another trail of adventure. The abortive trip to Soho had been calculated to arouse his interest, in preparation for this recital.

'The body was naked when it was found,' Herrington went on, 'and there were no obvious means of identification. It was little more than a skeleton. But we finally discovered who he was from the fillings in his teeth. We had them photographed, and managed to locate a dentist in London who had attended to him. The dentist gave us his address, and we found that his wife was still living there. Before we called on her we checked his name on our Missing Persons list. He'd been missing for nine months, and according to the pathologist must have been dead about that length of time, as I said.'

'What did his wife say?' Peter asked, gathering up Herrington's glass and replenishing it.

'She couldn't give us much assistance,

I'm afraid. She was very upset, of course. But, among other things, she mentioned Shirley Quentin. It seems that Stroud talked in his sleep, muttering this girl's name — and the old lady with a bustle.'

'Talked in his sleep, eh!' He made a grimace. 'A dangerous habit. There, Herrington, you have the reason why I have never married. How did his wife react to this nocturnal mumbling?'

'Just as you might expect. She wasn't bothered about the old lady, but Shirley was an entirely different matter. And as Stroud had been keeping very odd hours, saying he was working late at his office, which she found wasn't true, she began to think he was having an affair. Then to cap everything he was away from home for three days just before he disappeared.'

'H'm . . . And Shirley Quentin. You've located her, I suppose. What had she to say?'

Herrington took his pipe from his mouth, staring at it.

'Nothing yet. She lives in London, but she's out of town. I understand she's been staying with some friends in Devon and is returning tonight. Her father, a D.Sc. now retired, has a castle in Scotland — in Perthshire. Before she took a flat in London she used to live there with him. A bleak old place, I believe, called Castle Dreich. But that's by the way.'

Peter made a mental note of the name — as his visitor fully intended he should, though Castle Dreich was merely a distant link in the chain, as Herrington well knew.

'On the day Stroud disappeared,' he went on, 'he phoned his wife. At the time he was driving down the A1. Then, later, soon after he arrived home he left the house to get something he said he'd left in his car. That was the last his wife saw of him. But that very same night someone broke into his house. A desk in which Stroud kept some private papers relating to his work was rifled. Nothing else was touched. The burglar, I may say, was never caught.'

He finished his whisky and got to his feet.

'Well, I must be on my way. Pity you didn't have any luck in Soho.'

'A great pity,' Peter said, and left it at that as he saw his visitor to the front door.

'Anyway, thanks for your co-operation. I felt you were entitled to some explanation, though this case is purely an official matter, of course.'

'Yes, of course. I wouldn't think of butting in further on my own account.'

He closed the door after Herrington, returning slowly to the lounge, a twisted smile on his lips.

'So you're up to your old tricks, brother,' he muttered, a wicked gleam in his keen blue eyes. 'You don't kid me. You need unofficial assistance and I'm supposed to provide it. I wonder what the game is this time?'

3

It was not in Gayleigh's nature to disappoint anyone who dangled the prospect of adventure before him. Often it had been done quite openly and seldom for his own good, but he had always accepted the challenge, even though he knew he was treading a dark and unfamiliar path and presenting an unguarded chin.

Shirley Quentin ... Castle Dreich ... Mrs. Stroud. He considered each of these as a possible starting point, and there could be no doubt that the most likely and accessible source of further information was Mrs. Stroud. Her address would be in the telephone directory. He had provided himself with this information when his man, Carver, came to remove the breakfast things next morning.

'I notice you've put out my striped pants,' Peter remarked. 'Put 'em away, Carver. I shan't be wearing them today.'

'Indeed, sir. May I ask why?' He was an intensely loyal but somewhat wooden little man, inclined to take such remarks very literally.

'Because I intend to call on a lady.'

Carver's eyebrows lifted the merest trifle.

'I take it you will be wearing some other trousers, sir.'

'I hope so,' said Peter lightly. 'In the

best circles one doesn't make calls in one's underpants. The navy-blue suit will be more appropriate I think.'

There was no trace of the immaculate Peter Gayleigh when he called on Mrs. Stroud an hour later. He was wearing an old raincoat, shoes which were almost but not quite shabby, and a deferential expression — a detective making further inquiries.

Ethel Stroud, he found, was a colourless woman in her early thirties; her black dress accentuating her pale complexion.

'I really can't see how I can be of further help,' she said with listless resignation. 'I told Superintendent Herrington all I know.' Sadly and with some bitterness, she added: 'My husband didn't take me into his confidence.'

'So I understand, madam.' His tone was sympathetic. 'But he was a Civil Servant. So possibly his work was of a secret nature.'

She gave a wry smile. 'I very much doubt it. I should like to think he wasn't going around with another woman, but sometimes I found it difficult to believe.'

There was an awkward pause.

'I suppose his manner changed towards you, Mrs. Stroud?' Peter prompted, but she shook her head.

'No, he was just as considerate as he'd always been, except for his comings and goings. You'll know about those and that he gave me some very feeble excuses. Then when he began to talk in his sleep — '

'He kept repeating a certain phrase, I believe — 'The old lady with a bustle'.'

She raised her chin slightly, her face suddenly taut.

'And this woman's name — Shirley.'

'He said nothing else?' Peter pursued hurriedly.

'Nothing I could make out — it was mostly just muttering.' She was silent for a moment. 'But when he kept repeating 'The old lady with a bustle,' he didn't run the words together like that. He always paused in the middle. 'The old lady — with a bustle,' You see what I mean. Not that it's of much importance, I suppose.'

Peter considered this for a few

moments. Then: 'When your husband arrived here on the day he disappeared was he carrying anything with him?'

'Only his brief-case.'

'Containing papers which he locked away in his desk?'

'Yes, I suppose so. At any rate he went into his study. His brief-case was found empty after the robbery.'

'H'm. How long did your husband stay in his study?'

'Oh, a couple of minutes perhaps — not much longer.'

'Then he told you he was going to the garage to get something he'd left in his car.'

'Yes.'

'When he didn't come back I expect you went to the garage yourself?' And as she inclined her head: 'Did *you* find anything he might have left behind?'

'Nothing that mattered very much,' she told him with a shrug. 'Just the barograph. It was lying on the back seat.'

Peter frowned. 'The barograph?'

'Yes. I told Superintendent Herrington about that.'

Keeping his thoughts to himself, Peter said: 'He must have forgotten to mention it to me.'

'Well, it can't be important, really,' she said. 'Vincent kept it in the house instead of a barometer. We've had it for years, but neither of us bothered much about it. Then he got an idea. He said it might be used to check up on gradients, or something. He was always fond of carrying out little experiments.' She shook her head vaguely. 'I haven't a scientific mind, and I never understood what he meant. Anyway, he put the barograph in the car before he set off.'

'And it was there when he returned three days later.' Peter rubbed his chin thoughtfully. 'Mr. Herrington took the barograph chart away with him, I suppose?'

'No, it's in the study, together with the old ones.'

Trust Herrington — if 'trust' was the right word! That Herrington had failed to grasp its importance he didn't believe for one moment. Oh no! That wily policeman was much too astute.

Without doubt he had left it there for his stooge to find. Not for the first time Gayleigh felt a great admiration for Chief-Superintendent Herrington.

'May I take a look at those charts, Mrs. Stroud?'

'Certainly.' She crossed to the room door. 'If you'll come this way . . . '

The study was across the hall, the barograph standing very conspicuously beside a small pile of used charts on the desk. Herrington had made quite sure that it wouldn't be overlooked! The chart lying on top of the others showed the atmospheric pressure during the three days that Vincent Stroud had been away from home.

Peter gazed down at the inked record traced by the pen when it had moved over the paper, which had been attached to the circular drum of the barograph. During the early part of that week, before Stroud had set off on his mysterious journey, the record showed little change in the atmospheric pressure. But at eight o'clock on Tuesday morning the pen had begun to move tremblingly over the paper. And throughout that night the air pressure had evidently varied to an astonishing extent, the ink markings zig-zagging up and down.

These oscillations ceased early on Wednesday morning. Then early on Friday morning the pen had begun to zig-zag again. Peter realised the trembling of the pen had been caused by the vibration of Stroud's car. The zig-zag lines could not have recorded such violent changes in the weather. What then? His pulse racing faster he believed he had the answer. Barometric pressure, he reminded himself, changed according to altitude . . .

'I should like to keep this chart, Mrs. Stroud,' he said, and she raised no objection, though obviously puzzled.

'You think it's important?'

'Yes, I think it's very important,' he told her. 'And I'm quite sure Mr. Herrington knew that it was.'

'I simply don't understand,' she said, even more puzzled. 'If it is, why did he just leave it here?'

Peter shrugged non-committally.

'I don't know. Why not ask him next time he calls?'

He left with the certain feeling that she would do just that, finding it amusing to picture Herrington's attempts at evasion. Because he might find it difficult to answer that question.

But he would certainly realise that his stooge was well and truly on the job.

4

'Don't let me disturb you,' said Diana tartly. 'But just in case you've forgotten, I'm the girl you promised to take to lunch. Remember?'

Peter looked round vaguely, still absorbed in his thoughts.

'What's that? Do I remember what?'

Diana sighed. She had been waiting in the Jermyn Street flat for nearly half an hour, very conscious that her grey costume was the last word in chic, that the ultra fashionable hat showed off her corn colour hair to perfection and that Peter had scarcely noticed she was there.

He had greeted her with a brief nod when she had arrived, told her to take a pew and to keep silent.

'Because, my sweet, I have a problem to solve. Strange as it may seem I am doing a spot of hard thinking.'

And because Diana Caryll had been associated with him for so long she had obeyed meekly, passing the time by disposing of a couple of martinis. He could be extremely aggravating at times, she thought, so utterly self-sufficient.

'I might be less impatient,' she said, 'if you'd tell me what you're doing.' She was eyeing the open maps and the books on the table where Peter was sitting.

'For once I'm doing what our friend Herrington expected me to do,' he told her, looking up with a chuckle.

'It sounds too good to be true!'

'He thinks I might be useful to him. Just why, is beyond me at present.'

'But if I know anything, you'll find out,' Diana retorted with absolute conviction.

'Thanks for your touching faith in me, my sweet.' He eyed her silently for a moment, taking in her attractive appearance. 'Now you'd better trot along home and change into some more suitable clothes. Tweeds, I think, would be appropriate.'

'Peter!'

'You and I are going places.'

'How right you are,' she said firmly. 'We're going to lunch.'

'Of course if you're so dead set on it, we *could* eat first,' he conceded, and Diana gave a significant sniff.

'We're definitely going to. And now that's settled why have you been studying all those maps and things?'

He picked up the barograph chart. 'This,' he informed her, 'is Exhibit A. Just to work up your appetite for lunch I'll regale you with a mental aperitif — the story of the decayed body in the cellar.' And he launched into a resumé of his conversations with Herrington and Mrs. Stroud.

'With the result that I have this chart,' he concluded. 'Of course you realise that apart from the weather and the atmospheric pressure there's quite a lot to be learned from it.'

Diana peered at it again with a puzzled frown. 'No, I'm damned if I do.'

'Too bad!' He wagged his head. 'Somehow I didn't think you would. Between ourselves, I feel I'm pretty smart to have thought of it myself. As you know, modesty has never been one of my failings.'

'And how!' she confirmed, with a grimace.

Peter brought his cigarette to a glowing brightness, drawing the smoke deep into his lungs.

'Let's go back a bit. You remember I said that Stroud phoned his wife while returning home along the A1.'

'Huh-huh.' She nodded.

'Before that he'd thrown a spanner into the conjugal works by repeating Shirley Quentin's name in his sleep. And according to Herrington — who hasn't told me all he knows by a long chalk — her esteemed papa has a baronial domain, Castle Dreich, in Perthshire. Also I happen to know that Shirley

Quentin is engaged to Alan Sinclair who is at present living at Bridge of Allan, near Stirling. You see how the Scottish *motif* occurs throughout. Bearing that in mind, how would you interpret Stroud's second refrain: 'The old lady with a bustle'?'

'I can't interpret it,' she told him promptly. 'I haven't your colossal brain. But I can see you're just aching to tell me.'

Peter shot her a knowing glance, then pulled an open atlas towards him, pointing to a map of Scotland.

'There she is — the old lady herself!' he said triumphantly.

Diana stared at the map blankly.

'I'm sorry. I just don't get it.'

'No? That's because you're looking at Scotland as a whole, not merely part of it. Now look at this.'

From between the pages of the atlas he took a sheet of transparent paper on which he had traced part of the Scottish coastline. At the top he had written the words:

THE OLD LADY WITH A BUSTLE

'You see?' he went on. 'The county of Sutherland gives us the head and face, and Caithness the old lady's poke bonnet.' He outlined them with his finger. 'The islands of Skye and Mull represent her hands, which I'll admit are rather crude, but Moray, Banff, Aberdeen, and Kincardine form an excellent bustle, and Fife the foot.'

'Why, of course!' she exclaimed, her face lighting up. 'Though I must say it looks a bit like one of Walt Disney's hens, too.'

'That,' said Peter, 'is entirely irrelevant. We are not talking about hens. We are talking about the old lady with a bustle, or rather, the old lady — with a bustle. Mrs. Stroud mentioned that pause as an afterthought, but I've a hunch it's important. I've got an idea about that, too, but whether it's correct or not, the old lady brings us back to Scotland. And as Stroud was driving south it occurred to me that he might have been on his way from there.'

'He might.' She pursed her lips. 'But isn't that assuming rather a lot?'

'Perhaps.' He picked up the barograph chart, eyeing it reflectively. 'But now I've proved that he was.'

'From that chart?'

'Huh-huh.'

Diana was silent for a moment. 'You know I've a feeling you're going to give me a frightfully involved explanation,' she said. 'And I don't really know what a barograph is?'

'A barograph is simply a recording

barometer. It records the weather from the changes in air pressure. Fortunately the weather was extremely good when Stroud made his little trip, so in the ordinary way the inked line wouldn't have moved up and down very much. The reason it did was because the barograph was in Stroud's car, and recording all the changes in atmospheric pressure as he rode up hill and down dale. See what I mean?'

She considered this. 'Y-es,' she said slowly, 'you mean the air pressure changes according to the height above sea level.'

'Exactly. And as a gradient map gives that, all I had to do was compare, or pinpoint, the gradients on the A1 etc., with the peak points on the chart. That, of course, is what Stroud himself meant to do after he returned home. It was a very pretty little experiment, and I've no doubt he took every precaution to make it a success. For one thing his barograph was larger than most, the record on this chart correspondingly large, so it's not difficult to discover the route he took.

'Admittedly, there aren't many gradients on the A1. In that respect it was a very poor route. But beyond Lockerbie up to Beattock Summit there's a very marked rise, and it's quite easy to determine that on the chart. Then the height above sea level drops before Lanark, and drops still more at Stirling where I fancy he went.' He put a finger on the chart. 'Stirling would be about here.'

'Where the line stops dithering,' she said.

'No, just a little before that. Obviously he drove a few miles beyond Stirling. And wherever it was, he stayed there until early on Friday morning. You'll notice the second series of oscillations are exactly the same as the first, but in reverse order. Which means he took the same route back, and arrived home at — ' He bent a little closer. 'Yes, at approximately 9.30 on Friday night.'

'It's quite a fascinating game, isn't it,' Diana said. 'I must say you're pretty smart, darling.'

'Thanks. Herrington, of course, left this chart to lure me on. I'll bet he knows where Stroud actually went.'

'Could it have been to Castle Dreich, do you think?'

Peter shook his head.

'No, I've checked that. Castle Dreich is in the hills much further north. But he gave me Shirley Quentin's name, too, remember, and I'm pretty sure he realised I'd associate it with Alan Sinclair. Herrington's a sly devil all right! I haven't seen Sinclair since the engagement was announced, but as I told you, he has a place near Bridge of Allan.'

'And that's near Stirling,' Diana said brightly.

'Yes. Now you see the tie-up.'

She nodded, her face alive with interest.

'So we go north. In the Jaguar, I suppose?'

'To Bridge of Allan.' He got decisively to his feet. 'We'll put up at Carlisle for the night and tootle along to Sinclair's place in the morning. I'll get Carver to put up some grub. We can lunch alfresco on the way. The sooner we set off the better.'

Diana looked at him hard. She said dryly, 'Since I'm to be done out of a decent lunch in town you *will* give me time to change?'

'Of course.' There was a twinkle in his eye. 'I don't want to rush you.' And as a seeming afterthought: 'I say, that's a marvellous hat you're wearing. I've just noticed it.'

Breathing heavily she said with resignation: 'I'm wearing a new suit too. And it was all for your benefit. I really don't know why I bother.'

2

1

'Hadn't we better phone Alan Sinclair — to let him know we're coming?' Diana said next morning. They were breakfasting in Carlisle, after the long drive north.

'No, I think we'll just drop in out of the blue. I hope he'll put us up for a night or two, but if we let him know beforehand he might go to too much trouble.'

She smiled, shaking her head. 'That,' she said, 'is the smoothest bit of dissimulation I've heard — even from you. So you don't want your friend to know that we're coming. Are you afraid he'd try to put us off?'

Peter cocked his head on one side, his expression quizzical.

'Well — the thought did occur to me,' he admitted.

'Because you think he might have something to hide?'

'That's putting it rather strongly, Di. But Alan was always a rum sort of cove, inclined to be secretive. And as the late Mr. Stroud had the same failing, and they probably knew each other, we can't be too careful.' He glanced at his watch. 'H'm, it's about time we were pushing along.'

It was approaching noon when they reached Stirling, where history stared down at them from the castle, set like a buttress above the town, casting its spell over the quaint houses and cobbled side streets. Soon they were heading towards the Ochils; past the tiny village of Causewayhead, the sun transforming the twists and turns of the Forth into a shimmering ribbon of blue; past the thickly wooded slopes of Abbey Craig on their right and the Wallace monument, a majestic sentinel, its architectural crown riding on the puffs of cloud.

'Bridge of Allan,' Peter announced, as they came to a stretch of well built modern houses, including several hotels flanked by fir-clad hills. At the end of the main street they stopped to inquire the way, learning that Sinclair's house was about half a mile farther on. It was, they found, in an isolated position, very old, and surrounded by fir trees in which a multiplicity of crows had built their nests. The air seemed to be filled with the brush of wings and discordant cawing.

Peter brought the car to a standstill, surveying the grim, solid outlines of the house. 'Not what you might call a desirable summer residence,' he observed. 'Alan must have changed quite a bit.'

Diana wrinkled her nose. 'Old fashioned curtains, and all the windows shut.'

They went up a short path to the front door, Peter pulling an old-fashioned bell. It evoked a metallic shuddering from somewhere inside.

Diana looked at him in some dismay.

'Just the ghost dragging its chains, sweetheart,' he said. 'Anyway, the bell works, which is more than I expected.'

'What a place!' she deplored. 'By the look of it I bet it doesn't even sport a bath.'

Peter chuckled. 'Aren't you a bit previous. We haven't been received into the clan yet. I hope there's someone at home.'

The sound of footsteps told them there was. A key turned in the heavy lock. Then the door was opened by a tall, angular woman, dressed in black. Her grey hair was drawn back into a tight bun at the back of her head, and her face might have been chiselled out of granite.

'Good morning. Is Mr. Sinclair at home?' Peter asked.

'He is not,' the woman said bluntly.

'H'm, how unfortunate. I was passing this way and hoped to see him. I'm an old friend.'

'Aye. Then he's no' expectin' ye.'

'Er — no. But as I expect he'll be back shortly do you mind if we come in and wait for him?'

'If ye're so anxious tae see him ye'll hae to wait in yer car,' was the unbending response. 'I'm Mr. Sinclair's hoosekeeper, and I've been telt tae admit nabody.'

The door was closed in their faces and they were left staring at each other foolishly. The cawing of the crows seemed to swell into a derisive crescendo.

'A dour auld wifey if ever there was one,' Peter remarked.

Diana said, 'Well, she certainly knows her own mind. And we've come over four hundred miles for this! For heaven's sake give me a cigarette.'

Peter obliged, lighting one himself. They were walking slowly back to the car when he paused again, half-pointing.

'We're in luck! There's Sinclair now.'

Following the direction of his gaze she saw a man in breeks and an old slouch hat coming towards them. He was tall and lean, moving with the effortless stride of the habitual hiker.

'Hullo, Gayleigh!' he exclaimed, as he came up. 'You're the last person I expected to see. What brings you up here?'

It was not, Diana thought, an exuberant greeting, lacking genuine heartiness. His features, which were as brown as his hands, were sharp and gaunt, his very pale eyes deep set.

'We've been doing a spot of touring,' Peter said, as they shook hands. He introduced Diana. 'I don't think you two have met.'

She felt her hand crushed between strong, hard fingers.

'How do you do, Miss Caryll. I've heard Peter speak about you, of course.' The deep, pale eyes bored into her. 'I must apologise for my housekeeper. Mrs. Jamieson's a queer old stick. I noticed she wasn't very civil.'

Dour she might be, Peter thought, but she had simply been obeying instructions. Sinclair's instructions. As he preceded them to the front door he produced a key, fitting it into the lock, Peter wondering if the windows were locked, too. Obviously Sinclair spent most of his time out of doors, a man who liked fresh air, yet kept every window tightly shut. It seemed as unnatural as the hard-faced housekeeper.

He caught a glimpse of Mrs. Jamieson at the far end of the hall as they entered. But the woman quickly effaced herself, and without comment Sinclair took them into a sitting-room full of heavy mahogany furniture. It had the atmosphere and very tidy appearance of a room that was seldom used.

'We're rather old fashioned in these parts,' he said, as he saw them looking around in some surprise. 'Excuse the mid-Victorianism. I only rent this place, and haven't got around yet to looking for another.'

'I suppose you liked the situation,' Peter said, who felt there was nothing else anyone could have liked about this house.

'Er — yes. Now I expect you could both use a drink. What'll it be?'

Diana having expressed a preference for sherry, he produced a bottle of wine from a cupboard, together with a whisky decanter and a soda syphon. When they were all supplied:

'It must be more than a year since I saw you, Peter. I suppose you're wondering what I'm doing up here? Well, actually, old man, I got a job with the Forestry Commission. The production and supply of timber, and all that. I'm on nodding acquaintance with quite a few of these fir trees round about. Good clean air and plenty of it. But never mind that. How's dirty old London?'

'Still dirty,' Peter said, 'though they're cleaning more of the buildings up. Di and I thought we'd get away from it for a bit. We've been touring around for nearly a week now.' He enlarged on this, Diana marvelling afresh at his flair for relating fictitious happenings with such detailed impressiveness. Then presently he said blandly: 'If it wouldn't be too much trouble we're hoping you'll be able to put us up for a night or two, Alan.'

Faced with the rather blunt suggestion Sinclair hesitated momentarily.

'Well, I'm afraid you might find this old place rather depressing — ' he was pointing out, not wishing to appear unhospitable, when Peter put in cheer-fully:

'Depressing? Not a bit of it. Quiet and restful — yes. It has an old world charm. Don't you think so, Di?'

She nodded dutifully. 'But if it isn't convenient we don't want to impose on you, of course,' she said.

'No, of course not,' Peter said belat-edly, staring at him very straightly. And to Diana: 'I think I know how Alan feels.

He's afraid this old place lacks some of the amenities to which you might be accustomed, my sweet.'

'Yes, that's just it,' Sinclair turned to her. 'For one thing we haven't even a proper bath, only a primitive metal affair. I really think — '

'Oh, don't worry about that,' Diana said nobly. 'I'm not a bit finicky about such things.'

It was not the moment, Peter felt, to meet her eye. Giving Sinclair no time to make further excuses, he said smoothly: 'You see? She doesn't mind a bit. We shall manage all right. Much more matey than staying at a hotel.'

'Yes, of course.' Sinclair's reply was more than a trifle forced. Evidently he had realised that further prevarication would seem churlish. 'We have a couple of spare bedrooms, so we can easily put you up. I'd better tell Mrs. Jamieson that you'll be staying.'

He excused himself and went out, Diana shooting a significant glance at Peter as soon as he had gone.

'No bath!' she exclaimed bleakly. 'I just knew it!'

'All in a good cause, Di. Thanks for backing me up.'

'But really, Peter, how could you be so pushy? It was pretty clear he didn't want us to stay here.'

He looked at her with a half-impish, half-quizzical smile.

'Surely not? I didn't notice it.'

'Then you must be blind.'

'No, simply curious. In London he was quite a man about town, though he never told me much about what he was doing. I certainly didn't think he was interested in forestry. Yet now — '

He left the rest of his thoughts unsaid.

2

On renewed acquaintance, Mrs. Jamieson still maintained her dour, disapproving attitude. She said nothing beyond what the merest politeness demanded as Sinclair introduced his visitors, and as she showed them upstairs to their rooms. These overlooked the town, with the Wallace monument in the distance, Peter noticing that the old-fashioned windows were equipped with very modern locks.

Though he didn't remark on this, Sinclair, who had accompanied his housekeeper, had a ready explanation.

'We think it advisable to keep all the windows tightly shut,' he said. 'There were some burglaries in the town not so long ago. Not that we've anything worth pinching, but it's better to be careful than sorry.' He glanced at his wrist-watch. 'Now how about lunch? Mrs. Jamieson tells me she can soon knock something up for the three of us.'

'Aye. But it'll no be ready for aboot an hoor,' the woman said ungraciously.

Diana mustered her sweetest smile.

'I'm afraid we're putting you to an awful lot of trouble, Mrs. Jamieson.

'Aye, ye are a bit,' was the candid response. She indicated a clean towel she had placed over the rail of the old-fashioned washhandstand, eyeing Diana with a hard, straight stare. 'Ye'll be takin' a wash, nae doot.'

Not very sure whether this was a reminder or a suggestion Diana looked at herself quickly in the dressing-table mirror, somewhat to Peter's amusement.

'Thank you, Mrs. Jamieson,' she said. 'After the drive this morning I *should* like to tidy up.'

Later, and during the improvised meal, Sinclair made no mention of his engagement to Shirley Quentin, though during the lengthy conversation he was given plenty of opportunity. Apparently he was under the impression that neither of his visitors had seen the announcement, and for some reason preferred to say nothing about it.

Which was rather surprising, Peter thought. All the more so as he had rented a house not all that far from her father's home — Castle Dreich — while she had moved to London. If they were still engaged, it seemed to be rather a queer arrangement.

During the general conversation Sinclair said very little about his work. If he had any professional knowledge of forestry it certainly wasn't apparent. He appeared to know little more about it than Peter did himself.

A black marble clock on the dining-room mantelpiece was striking two o'clock when he suggested they might like to see some of the surrounding country-side that afternoon.

'I could show you around, if you like,' he said. 'I got through most of my work this morning, so I'm pretty free at the moment.'

And so it was arranged, Sinclair leaving them soon afterwards to get out his car.

'I wonder,' Diana remarked musingly while they were alone. 'Do you really think he *is* employed by the Forestry Commission?'

'If he is,' Peter said dryly, 'he can't be a great acquisition. To my mind he's behaving very oddly altogether.'

'That woman, Mrs. Jamieson, Peter. She isn't simply dour. She looks as hard as granite to me. I shan't be at all sorry to leave this house.'

A ghost of a smile curved Peter's lips.

'And all its dark secrets, Di? Shame on you! Though I must say, the master of the hoose, seems to have no intention of leaving us to our own devices while we're

47

here. Or is he being belatedly very hospitable?'

It was a pleasant enough drive, taking in Dunblane, Callender and Strathyre, largely uneventful until they were returning by way of Loch Lubnaig.

Then suddenly Peter realised they were being followed. A leather-jacketed figure on a motor-bike kept appearing at infrequent intervals on the winding road behind them. And although they were driving slowly he made no attempt to pass.

Under the pretext of showing them more of the countryside Sinclair began to take a roundabout route, his gaze never far from the driving mirror. While keeping at considerable distance the man on the motor-bike seemed to prefer the same side roads.

Yes, Sinclair also knew they were being followed, though he made no mention of it.

The motor cyclist was still in the near distance when they reached Bridge of Allan, but had disappeared before they pulled up outside the house. As Peter and

Diana alighted Sinclair produced the key to the front door.

'Mrs. Jamieson told me she was going out,' he said. 'You can let yourselves in. I'll be with you as soon as I've put the car away.'

The garage, Gayleigh had noticed, was built on to the back of the house, a recent addition apparently, for it was of yellow brick, in marked contrast to the much older, weather-beaten stone. Sinclair drove his car on to the cinder track leading round the back, and was out of sight when Peter pressed the door key into Diana's hand.

'Carry on, my sweet. I'll join you in a minute or two.' And as she frowned slightly: 'Maybe he's just garaging his car — but somehow I wonder?'

He waved her towards the house, waited until she had gone inside, then slipped round quietly to the back. Sinclair, he saw, had now put the car away, but was not in sight. Presumably, he was still in the garage, and had closed the large double doors behind him. The garage had a window round the side, and

49

Gayleigh reached it in a matter of seconds, peering cautiously in.

Sinclair was now moving towards a telephone. But he didn't pick it up at once. There was a black metal box standing underneath a wooden bench with a length of flex leading from it. He plugged the flex into a socket. Then pressing one of two buttons on the telephone itself he lifted the receiver.

Gayleigh's eyes narrowed. He knew what the metal box was — a frequency changer. Sinclair was using a scrambler telephone!

Since the conversation promised to be interesting Peter Gayleigh had no intention of missing it. But the window was closed, and if he remained where he was he would hear nothing. He moved stealthily towards the garage doors. Although substantial they didn't fit together perfectly. Hopefully, he pressed an ear against the join, and Sinclair's voice came to him. The words were faint, but quite distinct, and evidently the connection had just been made.

'Gundersen? . . . Yes, Sinclair here. The old lady — '

He broke off, waiting expectantly, and Peter's eyes gleamed. The old lady — with a bustle! All along he had been pretty sure that it was being used as a code, and here was confirmation. So Alan Sinclair had been associated with Vincent Stroud. Had Stroud visited him during those three days that had not been accounted for? If so, what was behind all this secrecy? And who was Gundersen?

'Right,' Sinclair was saying. 'I'm switching over to the scrambler.'

There was a short pause. Then:

'Yes, I can hear you perfectly.'

He didn't speak again for some time, evidently listening intently.

'So you've achieved the final mutation,' he said presently. 'That's excellent. But listen, Gundersen. What I was afraid of has happened. They're creeping north. I was followed this afternoon by one of them on a motor-bike, so, for the time being, I'd better not see you at the castle.' There was another pause. 'Yes, until I've got rid of him. It's just possible he doesn't know anything much yet, but you'd better take precautions. And warn that half-wit Gregory. There may be more of the scum about. The man who tailed me was wearing a black leather jacket — '

So far he got when there was a dramatic interruption. A bullet ricochetted with a shrill whine from the brickwork near the garage window.

As Gayleigh jerked round the hidden marksman fired again. And this time there was the sound of splintering glass. Instinctively he darted back flattening himself against the garage doors, peering in the direction from which the shots had come. At first he saw no one. Nothing moved on the hilly countryside — until a man emerged from some trees near the road more than a quarter of a mile away. He was carrying a rifle, and wore a black leather jacket.

The man with the motor-bike. And from what Peter had seen of it, it was a very powerful machine. Pursuit he realised would be futile.

He edged round the side of the garage, back to the window. There was a neat, circular hole surrounded by splintered glass, and he wondered if Sinclair had been hit. A moment later he was peering inside again. The bullet had gouged a small crevice in the brick only a few inches from where Sinclair had been standing. Now he had replaced the phone and was disconnecting the frequency changer, well out of line from the window.

Peter waited no longer, moving swiftly back to the front of the house.

Diana had left the door unlatched, and as he ran quickly up the stairs he met her on the landing.

'Well?' she asked curiously. Evidently she hadn't heard the sound of the bullets or the splintering glass.

'Not here,' he said. 'Later.'

'You've been rather a long time,' she insisted. 'What's your mysterious chum doing?'

'I didn't ask him, Di. I expect he won't be a minute — but something tells me he won't be in the mood for light conversation. I don't think we should bother him for a bit. Guests can be very trying at times.'

He walked past her to his room, looking back in the doorway to give her a sly wink.

3

It could not be said that dinner was a hilarious meal. Sinclair did his best to appear at ease, but couldn't disguise the fact that he was worried. Not unnaturally, Peter thought, in view of what had happened. Sinclair was lucky to be alive! Soon after rejoining them in the house he had excused himself, saying that he had a report to finish connected with his work. They had seen very little of him before dinner.

In the meantime his housekeeper had returned, seemingly from a shopping expedition in Stirling, the outing having done nothing to dispel her dour reserve. Defeated in her well meant efforts to get on better terms with her, Diana gave it up, passing most of the time with Peter perusing the newspapers and a few magazines in the living-room, while the meal was being prepared. She had offered to help Mrs. Jamieson in the kitchen, but had been rebuffed.

The woman served the meal, which she referred to as 'High tea' as if she would not be sorry when they had gone, and though Peter did his best to enliven the conversation with a forced heartiness, Diana was very conscious of the effort Sinclair was making to be affable. She was more than glad when Peter suggested they might look round the town together before it got dark.

'I spotted quite a few likely-looking pubs,' he said. 'I suppose you've sampled all the local brews, Alan?'

'Er — yes. You two go right ahead. I'll make myself comfortable with a book.'

That, I very much doubt, Peter thought, and said so to Diana a quarter of an hour later after they had left the house.

'When we've strolled around for a bit to give the right impression, I think we might make our way quietly to yonder tree-clad hill. There are a few things I haven't told you, Di.'

She was following the direction of his

gaze, puzzled, as he added, 'If by any chance you should see a snooper attached to a motor-bike anywhere in the vicinity you might warn me before he plugs us in the back. So far he's only attempted to shoot Sinclair. But one never knows — this sportsman may get more ambitious.'

Her incipient frown deepened.

'Peter! What on earth are you talking about?'

'I'm talking about a leather-coated individual who tailed us this afternoon. On a motor-bike. I rather gathered he didn't like our host very much — he took a couple of pot shots at Sinclair while he was putting his car away. Or, to be more exact, while our enigmatic friend was doing a spot of phoning.'

As they walked on he told her what had occurred, adding briefly that he had overheard Sinclair's conversation, and pointing out the significance of the words: the old lady — with a bustle.

'He made very sure he was actually speaking to this man Gundersen before he switched to the scrambler. Who

Gundersen is, I don't know, but from his name he could be Norwegian. I gathered he was doing some sort of biological work — the word 'mutation' was mentioned. And it would seem that he's in the habit of meeting Sinclair at a castle. Possibly Castle Dreich. We'll do a spot of sightseeing in that direction tomorrow.'

Taking a circuitous route, mainly along field paths shielded by tall hedges, they made their way to the vantage point used by the sniper. There was no sign of him now. He had vanished long ago.

Peter led the way among the trees and bushes, halting at a spot that offered ample cover while presenting a good view of the house.

'I think we'll stay here for a while,' he said. 'Possibly we're wasting our time, but you never know. If nothing startling transpires we'll go along for a drink later. In the meantime, how about a cigarette?'

He had provided her with one when she said: 'I don't know what you hope to see. And just suppose someone passes this way and spots us. They'll wonder what on earth we're doing here.'

'You really think so?' He eyed her quizzically. 'I'm surprised at you, my sweet. A girl and a man enjoying rustic privacy. Have you no imagination?'

Diana looked at him, with a wry grimace.

'Well, I only hope we shan't have to play the part. I'm not used to being sexy in such surroundings — besides, this grass is wet.'

Peter chuckled. 'To revert to more apposite matters,' he said, 'I forgot to tell you about another bloke Sinclair mentioned over the phone. A man called Gregory. A half-wit, he called him, and though he was probably exaggerating I gather Mr. Gregory isn't overloaded with grey matter. Possibly a laboratory assistant or — ' He broke off suddenly, seizing her arm. 'Look!'

Sinclair had appeared at the back door of the house.

She was leaning forward to get a better view when Peter pulled her quickly back.

'Steady on! He's got a rifle.'

Diana froze. It had seemed that he was staring directly towards them. Hidden by

58

the trees again she asked anxiously: 'Is — is he coming this way?'

'No. At least, not yet. He's scanning the countryside. Keep out of sight, Di.'

For fully a minute her eyes remained fixed on Peter Gayleigh's lean, set face, as he continued to peer through an opening in the leafy branches.

'Well? What's he doing now?'

'Not to worry. He's gone into the garage. Take another look.'

Moving forward again she saw that he was blocking up the window with a stout board. It took some time before he had hammered it into position. Then he appeared again outside the garage. He was no longer carrying the rifle. He re-locked the double doors, and went back into the house.

'End of performance apparently,' Peter said. 'You know, I've a hunch this sniper laddie isn't going to have it all his own way. Things are developing, slowly.'

'Quite fast enough for me,' Diana retorted. 'What now?'

'That drink we promised ourselves, I think. I doubt if any more bullets will be flying just yet. But we mustn't be impatient. This is becoming quite interesting.'

Her reply lacked much of his own enthusiasm — all the more so as the heel of one of her shoes had sunk deeply into the soft earth, and she was busy extricating it. Life with Peter, she reminded herself, was never dull, if rather exacting at times. Particularly when he was interfering, as he usually was, in matters that did not concern him. He would never change, she thought, though in her heart she would not have had it otherwise. He was her man. And very much a man behind his debonair façade.

It was shortly after ten when they returned from the village, Sinclair admitting them. Mrs. Jamieson, it transpired, had already retired for the night.

'I usually keep fairly early hours myself,' he said, after they had chatted inconsequentially for a time. 'I expect to be pretty busy tomorrow, so I think I'll call it a day.'

'Yes, me too,' said Peter, looking at Diana, who nodded.

But in the seclusion of his room he made no attempt to undress. Unless he was greatly mistaken there would be more activity that night, and he had no intention of missing it. He had quite a lot to think about.

Apart from that day's events he had yet to find the motive behind Herrington's indirect approach. There could be no doubt that Herrington had foreseen that he would make this trip, though he couldn't be absolutely sure that he had meant him to visit Alan Sinclair. He had not mentioned his name, and the barograph chart had not revealed the end point of Stroud's journey north with great exactness. It had only provided a rough guide. Yet Herrington had surely known that it would lead him to somewhere in this locality. So what more natural than that he should call on Sinclair?

It might also be argued that Herrington had known Sinclair would bear watching. But if so, why hadn't he dealt with the matter himself, acting through official channels. There had been nothing whatever to suggest that Sinclair was under official observation — quite obviously the man with the motor-cycle had no connection with the police — yet Herrington had deliberately lured him, Peter, into this adventure. He was of course using him. But why? It was all the more puzzling since he was under no obligation to Herrington to reveal what he discovered.

He shrugged, lit a cigarette, and settled himself down to pass the time with a book he had brought with him. He was still very much awake when a distant clock chimed one a.m. And the notes had scarcely reverberated into silence when he heard the faint purring of a car. Sinclair's car. It was being driven as quietly as possible from the garage to the road, and as he listened intently the sound became fainter, receding into the distance.

He didn't stop to think where Sinclair had gone. It was sufficient that he had left. For in view of the precautions taken to make the house impregnable there must be something there, Peter argued, which would repay inspection.

He crossed to the door, opened it, and

stepped quietly out on to the landing. Then, with a cat-like tread, descended the stairs to the hall. The room where Sinclair had written his report!

He was moving in the direction when he heard the squeak of a floorboard coming from somewhere on the landing above. And a few moments later he heard it again as he stood there tense, striving to pierce the darkness. It could only be Diana or —

With sudden decision he felt for a light switch and snapped it on.

Mrs. Jamieson was standing at the head of the stairs, frowning. She was wearing a thick woollen dressing gown, and quite obviously had heard him leave his room.

Hiding his chagrin he simulated an expression of apologetic surprise. 'Oh, it's you, Mrs. Jamieson. I'm sorry if I disturbed you. I couldn't sleep, so thought I'd come down for a book.'

The woman continued to stare at him.

'Aye. Ye've no' been trying to sleep very hard, I'm thinking,' she said, in her blunt way. 'It's the wee sma' hoors, and ye've still got yer clothes on.'

'I've just finished a book I brought with me,' Peter improvised. 'I thought perhaps I could find another one.'

'Well, ye'ill no find one in that room.' Then with an expression of resignation: 'I'll just come doun and help ye mesel'.'

She joined him in the hall, accompanying him into the sitting-room. There was a bookcase there, and she stood over him as he made his choice. Having done so he felt obliged to return upstairs, feeling it would be foolish to leave his room again that night. Damn the woman!

With a wry glance at the book he tossed it on to a chair, and began to undress. But though he got into bed, dozing intermittently, the sound of Sinclair's car returning did not escape him. As it was driven quietly back into the garage he looked at his watch.

It was after four a.m.

3

1

Diana made the suggestion during breakfast, prompted by a significant glance from Peter. This was after Sinclair had told them he had business in Edinburgh that morning with a senior officer of the Forestry Commission.

'Peter and I thought we'd drive around doing some more sightseeing today,' she said. 'I've never been to this part of Scotland before, you know.'

'Then you must certainly see more of it. There's some very fine scenery you shouldn't miss.'

Though there were shadows under his eyes and tiny wrinkles of fatigue at the corners, his manner gave no indication that he had spent the greater part of the night without sleep. Wherever he had been it had evidently proved very satisfactory, for he was less on edge, more talkative than he had been the previous day.

He mentioned the beauty of the Ochils, outlining a route which would bring them back through Fife. And to further this suggestion he produced a road map indicating places of interest on the way. It was perhaps significant, Peter thought, that such a trip would take them in the opposite direction to Castle Dreich!

'Such well meant efforts!' he said dryly to Diana, after they had left in the Jaguar. 'It secms a pity to disappoint him, but the Ochils can wait.'

Having made some inquiries before returning to the house the previous night, they had learned exactly where the castle was situated. It was almost impossible to reach it by a public road, one approach being by way of Strathyre, some twenty odd miles from Bridge of Allan, on the road to Oban. From Strathyre they had decided to walk across the moor towards Ben Vorloch.

At the foot of the hill, Gayleigh swung the car round in that direction.

'Our friend Alan seemed less anxious

this morning,' he said, as they lit cigarettes. 'I daresay you noticed it.'

Diana settled herself more comfortably, expelling the smoke slowly.

'Yes. I was wondering about that. How do you account for it?'

'I can't, Di. But I know one thing — he must have made pretty good use of his time last night. Which is more than I did. That Jamieson woman has uncommonly sharp hearing.' And as Diana looked at him vaguely. 'She spotted me on the prowl.'

As the big car covered the miles he told her what had occurred. They had passed Dunblane and were nearing Doune when he came to the end of his recital.

'So Sinclair was away for more than three hours,' she said reflectively. 'You think he went to Castle Dreich?'

Peter shrugged. 'Perhaps. I don't know. When I heard him speaking on that scrambler phone he was certainly very keen to see what his pal Gundersen had accomplished. On the other hand he made it very plain that he wasn't going to the Castle until he'd got rid of the bloke on the motor-bike.'

Diana remarked that if he was still around they hadn't seen any sign of him that morning.

'No.' Peter rubbed his chin. 'I'm wondering if Alan took that rifle with him . . . Also I'm not at all happy about Mrs. Jamieson. She's not exactly partial towards us. And I don't think for one moment she was deceived when she caught me downstairs last night. Yet I've an odd feeling that she hasn't told Sinclair. If she has he's a damn sight better actor than I gave him credit for. We're staying with him on sufferance, of course, but I can't figure what he's up to at all.'

Beyond Callander the hills rose majestically on either side, wreathed in mist as they drove through the Pass of Leny, and by the banks of Loch Lubnaig to the tiny village of Strathyre. There was an immense silence in these parts, Diana noticed, as they went a little farther on in the direction of Balquhidder. But presently it was broken by the calling of plovers and the distinctive cry of a peewit.

In places the fir trees on the distant hills appeared as a threadbare carpet.

Scarves of cloud had wrapped themselves about the brow of the steeper patriarch ahead and as the car wound its way through the glen other peaks beyond crowded dimly in the distance, remote, serene guardians of the solitude. To their right the green hills were closer, acre upon acre of grassy moorland sloping away into the overcast sky.

Diana took a deep breath, expelling it slowly.

'Good moorland air,' said Peter. 'Impressed?'

'Mmm-Mmm,' She nodded, without looking at him. 'I was thinking of that wonderful metaphor of Walt Whitman's. About grass. 'The handkerchief of the Lord' he called it. I can appreciate that more than ever now.'

Peter's gaze rested on her reflectively.

'He also referred to it as 'the beautiful uncut hair of graves' which, to people like you and me, is not quite so soothing.'

'You don't think we're in danger.' she asked quickly, shaken out of her reverie.

'Not yet. We haven't been followed. But when we cross those desolate moors . . . A body might lie there for weeks without being discovered.'

Diana wrinkled her nose.

'Aren't you being rather morbid?'

'Possibly. It was just a thought.' The car began to slow down as his foot moved on the brake. 'About here, I think. This is were we start hiking.'

Having pulled up, he slipped the strap of a leather binocular case over his shoulder, then, producing a compass, took his bearings.

'East-north-east, is over there,' he said, pointing towards the hills on their right. 'If we head in that direction we ought to see Castle Dreich sooner or later. Pity it's such a dull day. Poor visibility.'

The ground was studded with bog-holes, and it was difficult to walk over the uneven tussocks. Presently they reached the brow of the nearest hill, only to find that the mist on the slopes beyond made it impossible to see far ahead.

Peter consulted the compass again.

'Come on. We've several miles to go

yet. If only this mist would clear a bit!'

Descending the slope, where chuckling burns and the cry of solitary birds were the only sounds, they came to another glen. Beyond this the ground began to rise again, and they had reached a broad shelf in the hills when Peter called a halt. Thankful for the rest, Diana sank down on to the heather while he surveyed the landscape through his field glasses. The mist had thinned in places, and hoping to get a better view he approached the edge of a crag, finding it overlooked a tiny loch which had been invisible on the way up.

He had lowered the glasses, peering down into the brackish water when his sharp eyes narrowed. Near the edge of the loch, where the steep escarpment sloped towards a narrow inlet, something protruded from the water. A piece of metal, glistening faintly, caught in a shaft of anaemic sunlight.

He levelled the glasses on it, frowning. No, he had not been mistaken. It was part of the handlebar of a motor-cycle.

Diana, who had come up behind him,

saw nothing unusual, eyeing him curiously.

'Take a look at that,' he said, pointing it out and handing her the glasses.

Wonderingly she raised them to her eyes, studying it for a few seconds. Then as she lowered them again:

'I can't think what it is. Can you?'

He made no direct reply. 'Let's take a closer look at it.'

The ground sloped down quite steeply towards the loch, the grass becoming soggy beneath their feet. Intent on avoiding the worst patches Diana was picking her way carefully with Peter's assistance, when he halted suddenly.

'My God!' He was staring down at the sparse grass immediately ahead of them.

Then she saw it too, her eyes widening.

It was a footprint. In some respects it resembled that of an ape, the impression being much deeper on the outside of the bare foot. The imprint of the toes was clearly defined. But there were only three of them!

As he bent down examining it closer she glanced back nervously over her shoulder. Nothing but silence, which seemed to have become more intense.

'I don't much like this, Peter,' she said.

'No, neither do I.' But as he straightened himself his strong face was set in an expression she knew so well. Keen interest coupled with the determination that would always lead him on to further endeavour, come what may. And here was something that added a spur to this quest.

The footprint pointed towards the edge of the crag, and he set off in that direction, hoping to find others. But he could detect only one more, faintly outlined, before the coarse grass merged into heather.

'Peter!' Her sharp exclamation jerked him round. After he had left her she had walked on a few paces. Now he saw she was pointing to the ground.

'Here's another one,' she called out. 'And another,' she repeated a few moments later.

He came quickly back to her. The prints she had found were pointing in the opposite direction to those he had already seen. Also they had made a deeper impression.

'Curiouser and curiouser,' he said. 'But one thing's clear, Di. The creature that made these footprints came round the crag over the heather, then later went back the same way.'

Diana nodded, staring down at them again, frowning.

'These prints are much more defined,' she remarked. 'Yet the ground isn't any damper here.'

'Yes . . . It looks to me as if he was carrying something pretty heavy.' His gaze went towards the small expanse of stagnant water, not far below them now. 'Unless I'm greatly mistaken that bit of metal glinting down there is part of a motor-bike.'

Diana blinked, staring at it again.

'You're not suggesting — ?' she was beginning when he interrupted her.

'That he could have been carrying it? No, I can't credit that. Let's press on.'

There were more of the footprints as they continued towards the loch. And they had almost reached it when they saw the impression of tyre marks on the soft earth. Those of a motor-cycle. The track emerged from some heather near the bank and leading up to it, where it disappeared abruptly. Obviously the machine had been wheeled into the water, some of the bare footprints showing alongside it.

Peter looked at Diana. Neither of them said anything.

Then as he moved ahead of her, peering down over the edge of the loch, his strong features tightened into a masklike rigidity.

Very apprehensively she came up to him — sucking in her breath sharply as she saw the face of the dead man.

2

It stared up at them, the eyes bulging, the tongue protruding horribly. The water was only a few feet deep, and they could see the rippling outlines of the body, held down by the framework of the motor-cycle, the upturned face only a few inches below the surface. The man was wearing a black leather driving jacket.

'Strangled!' Gayleigh muttered grimly.

Slowly, he shifted his gaze to the wind-swept carpet of heather behind them. Had there been a struggle there? He could see no sign of one.

'It looks to me as if he was carried for quite a distance before he was thrown into the water — and the motor-bike on top of him. Anyway, Sinclair doesn't need to worry any more!'

'Peter!' She had gone very pale.

'Not that I think he did this, of course. He's changed a hell of a lot, but I can't believe he'd have any part in a murder of this kind.'

He turned back, following the tracks of the heavy machine, into the heather. But on closer inspection the wiry, wind-swept roots revealed nothing.

'Hopeless, I'm afraid,' he said. 'No, our late departed doesn't seem to have met his fate anywhere near here. I'm wondering what became of the rifle he had with him yesterday. It wasn't in the water, as far as I could see. I'd better take another look at the body.'

'Not me,' she said emphatically, wrinkling her nose. 'I'll wait here.' Then as a sudden though struck her: 'I suppose we ought to report this.'

'And land ourselves in an official investigation? Not on your life. The body can stay where it is — after I've finished with it. There may be something in the pockets.'

It was a gruesome prospect, and she watched him in silence as he removed his shoes and socks and took off his jacket, rolling up his trousers and shirt sleeves before disappearing over the edge of the loch.

It was some five minutes later when he clambered back, rejoining her.

'Well?' she asked. She had been gazing about nervously.

'Not a thing. Not even any loose cash, or keys, on him. He's been frisked very thoroughly.'

'By this horrible creature that carried him down here?'

'It could be. Which denotes a considerable amount of intelligence.' His mouth quirked slightly. 'But no Frankenstein monster. It must have been a man — malformed, or maybe crippled — and certainly very strong.'

'A sort of Caliban, you mean.' She looked round apprehensively again. 'Well, whatever he is I hope he isn't still at large!'

'That's very unlikely, I think,' he told her reassuringly. 'Even if he's a half-wit he must have a home. And to my mind it's significant that he dealt with this motor-cyclist. Maybe he was obeying instructions. Anyway, it's too much to believe he goes about attacking everyone he meets. I think we're safe enough.'

'So we push on regardless,' she said. 'Oh yes, I know, you needn't tell me. All right I'm game.' And as she shot a glance in the direction of the dead man: 'The sooner we leave this spot the better I'll feel!'

He was already slipping on his jacket, and as soon as he had attended to his socks and shoes they set off again, meeting no one as they walked steadily on.

It was almost an hour later when they reached the top of a hill offering an excellent view of the surrounding moor. Behind them the loch with its grim secret had become a tiny circle of blue framed in the heather. Ahead, screened by a sprawling outcrop of rock, was the hard outline of Castle Dreich.

3

They came upon it suddenly, and though it was still more than half a mile away, Peter motioned Diana back behind the rock, before gazing at it through the binoculars.

It was set low in the hills, the architecture starkly unelaborated, except for four clover-shaped towers rising only a few feet about the main building of weathered grey stone. A wing jutted from this, a much lower and more modern structure, with a flat roof partly hidden by trees. There was a room in one of the squat towers, a narrow window commanding a full sweep of that part of the moor. Though he couldn't be certain he thought he could discern the head and shoulders of a man stationed there.

An iron stairway led up from the lower wing to this room, and he was still peering at it when a faint but unmistakable sound broke the still silence. It came pulsating over the glen behind them. The note of a distant plane.

'Over there!' Diana exclaimed, crouching down as she pointed. 'And it's coming this way!'

As they watched, the tiny speck grew larger. A helicopter. And now it was losing altitude rapidly.

'It's going to land, or else fly over the loch, Peter. Do you suppose they'll see — ?' She broke off as he levelled his binoculars again.

'Only a few feet above the water now,' he told her. 'And there are two men in it. Oh yes, they're searching all right!'

The plane hovered for a time over the spot where, as near as he could judge, the body was lying. Then it began to ascend vertically above the loch.

'They've seen it,' she said tensely. 'They

must have done.'

'Yet they haven't landed to investigate.' The corners of his mouth tugged down. 'After all, what's a dead body!'

The helicopter was moving forward again. It was coming closer, but taking a route well away to their right, flying low now between the intervening hills. Crouching further back they watched it pass, still some distance away, the pilot and his passenger staring straight ahead.

The man at the controls was heavily built with a short grey beard and horn-rimmed glasses. And there was no mistaking the sharp profile of his companion.

It was Alan Sinclair.

The helicopter flew on out of sight, then very soon afterwards the sound of its motors ceased. It had landed on the low, flat roof of Castle Dreich.

Diana was about to peer round the outcrop of rock when Peter thrust out a restraining hand. 'Careful, Di! Not yet — there's someone in that watch tower . . . Ah!'

Even without the glasses she could see

what had prompted his exclamation as he beckoned to her. An indistinct figure was descending the iron stairway, evidently about to join the other two, now stepping from the stationary machine. Through the binoculars Peter saw that it was a man wearing a grey sweater and baggy, very shabby trousers. His stocky build together with the breadth of his shoulders and barrel-shaped chest, gave the impression of immense strength. The short legs were bowed, his feet bare, his ungainly movement down the stairway resembling that of a gorilla.

He approached the other two hesitantly as they waited for him, both staring in his direction. Then the bearded man stepped towards him, gesticulating. Some words were evidently being exchanged, the bow-legged man spreading his hands, as if apologetically, the broad shoulders drooping. It seemed that he had been severely reprimanded when all three of them moved out of sight behind the intervening trees. A few moments later, the helicopter began to descend through the roof.

Obviously it had been standing on some type of lift.

It had disappeared completely when the bow-legged man came into sight again. He was alone now, waddling with his peculiar gait back to the iron stairway. He went up it and into the watch tower.

'Back on guard duty,' Peter muttered. And as he cast a meaning glance at Diana: 'Strong as a bull, by the look of him. I wouldn't like to meet him on the moor at night.'

'Neither would I,' she said quietly, sharing his thoughts.

'I'm inclined to think he could be the man called Gregory. Over the phone Sinclair referred to him as a half-wit, you remember.'

She nodded, frowning. 'And the older man with the beard could be Gundersen.'

'Yes, I'd say so. He certainly isn't Dr. Quentin. I've never met Quentin, but I've seen him on TV. He has an international reputation. I can't see him being mixed up in this sort of thing — even if his daughter is.'

'And Sinclair.'

'Yes.'

Was Quentin still living at the castle? If not, where was he? Surely no harm could have come to him, for Sinclair was his prospective son-in-law? Also, his daughter had been associated in some way with Vincent Stroud, who had known the code words 'The old lady — with a bustle.'

So Sinclair, Shirley Quentin, and Stroud had all been working together. So it was inconceivable that Dr. Quentin himself wasn't aware of it — an eminent man who wouldn't stoop to anything illegal. Which, Peter thought, got him absolutely nowhere. All the vital pieces in this jigsaw were still missing.

Though they waited for several minutes neither Sinclair nor the bearded man appeared again. Apparently they had left the roof, and gone into the building.

'Well, what now?' Diana said with a shrug. 'I don't fancy sneaking up any closer — not with Caliban on the job!'

'No, there could be difficulties.'

'I'll say! Frankly I've seen quite enough of Castle Dreich. And if it wasn't for that good Scottish breakfast I should be famished. So I vote we start walking back. We've covered quite a few miles as it is. Unless you want Sinclair to know what we've been up to, it's the only sensible thing to do.'

Since he could find no argument against this, he agreed.

'I'm feeling a bit peckish too,' he said as they set off on the long walk back.

As there was room for much speculation the return journey was not as tedious as it might have been. But it was well into the afternoon when they reached the Jaguar, Diana sinking down into it thankfully.

'I don't care if I never see your Scottish moors again,' she said wearily, easing her slim legs and moving her aching feet. 'All I want is some food.'

'That,' said Peter, as he let in the clutch, 'seems a tolerably good idea.'

4

The meal in Strathyre was simple enough, but very satisfying. It consisted of a generous helping of bacon and eggs rounded off with Scotch pancakes and honey.

'How do you feel now?' Peter asked, when they had finished.

'If you really want to know,' she said. 'I feel like sitting here and never moving again.'

'Bad for your figure, Di.' His eyes twinkled. 'It's early yet, so what do you say to another little walk presently?' And as he caught her look of dismay: 'Nothing very strenuous, my sweet. But this is a temperance hotel, so in due course I think we might push on to an inn I spotted just down the street . . . '

As he had hoped, the landlord of the inn, a local Scot, proved to be very knowledgeable. In the tiny bar parlour, with drinks at their elbows they drew him into casual conversation, before referring to Castle Dreich with what appeared to be no more than mild interest.

It was very old, he told them, parts of it dating back to the thirteenth century. It was even said that William Wallace had stayed there after recapturing it, together with most of the fortresses north of the Forth, from the English in 1297, and only a few months before the battle of Stirling.

'But a cauld, dreich place,' he added. 'I'm no surprised the Doctor was aye bletherin aboot it.' He wagged his head, sucking at a pipe. 'I dinna ken what has become of him and his wee lassie. I hae nae seen either o' them for a year noo.'

It transpired that he had a great admiration for Doctor Quentin who had called at the inn occasionally since purchasing the castle some ten years ago.

'He's a fine man, but the moor's nae place for yon bright wee lassie. She was aye wantin' to go away to London. And why not, says I? She's young and entitled to her bit pleasure. She comes here verry seldom noo, though I believe she visits her faither mair often since the castle has been modernised a bit.'

The flat roof was a recent addition, they learned, and there had been other alterations carried out about a year before. But when they asked about these he was unable to give them any precise details.

'The Doctor has no said muckle aboot it tae me,' he explained. 'Likely the castle is much better noo. But, och, the man wasna wise to wait sae long.'

So his daughter visited him occasionally. Which was very kind of her, Peter thought sardonically! Provided, of course, that her father was still living there. If he wasn't, which seemed very possible, where had he gone?

Well, his footloose daughter must know — and seemingly a lot of other things too. And now that he had covered the preliminary ground, the sooner he made her acquaintance the better, though there was every indication she would be as tight mouthed as Sinclair.

Dust had masked the hills when they bade the landlord farewell, the deeper hush of night settling over the countryside as they drove back to Bridge of Allan.

Sinclair had already returned, his manner towards them affable, though somewhat restrained. Once again Peter gave him an entirely fictitious account of their exploits that day, being careful to avoid too much detail. It was evidently expected of him, Sinclair listening with interest.

'Mrs. Jamieson got a telegram this evening,' he remarked presently. 'Her sister in Glasgow has been taken ill. Nothing very serious, we hope, but she'll be leaving to visit her tomorrow. I don't know how long she'll be away, of course.'

The hint was unmistakable, and Peter took it. Partly because it fitted in very nicely with his own decision.

'I understand, old man. It's going to make things a bit difficult.'

'Well — er — yes.'

'Not to worry,' said Peter. 'Diana and I were just going to tell you — we have to be back in London tomorrow anyway.'

To do him justice Sinclair looked rather embarrassed, they thought, muttering something apologetically about his seeming lack of hospitality, which both of them stoutly denied, their insincerity matching his own.

They retired shortly afterwards, Diana falling asleep almost immediately, Peter mulling over the facts he had gleaned, Sinclair with the nagging conviction that

Gayleigh's visit had not been fortuitous. There was, he felt sure, a definite reason behind it. And if that was so, who had inspired him? Where had he got the information that had brought him to Bridge of Allan?

There must, Sinclair argued, have been a leakage somewhere. Which was more than disconcerting, for there were others concerned in this project whose activities might be jeopardised. In London! Maynard and Eidervik were there — and Shirley. He must warn Shirley before Gayleigh started sticking his nose in further. Why the hell couldn't he mind his own business, but that, he reflected, was not in Peter Gayleigh's nature.

How much did this interloper know? Where had be been during the past two days? Sinclair was under no delusion that he had been told a pack of lies, and with Gundersen's object almost achieved . . .

He thought of Vincent Stroud, as he had done many times during the past months. The man had been a fool to visit him in Scotland. He had paid for this mistake with his life, but the repercussions seemed to be endless.

That body in the loch! Under his breath he cursed Gregory. An excellent watch-dog, but in some ways unpredictable. The man had been a fool to leave the body there. In his mind's eye he saw Gregory removing it from its unfortunate resting place, and staggering across the moor, under cover of darkness, to the grave dug in readiness near Castle Dreich that afternoon. He must phone Gundersen tomorrow to make sure this had been carried out. This motor cyclist wouldn't be the last one to spy on them he was sure. There would be others sent to replace him.

With the feeling that disaster was pressing closer there was little sleep for Sinclair that night.

In the morning Peter, supported by Diana, said all the correct things expected of departing guests. With equal insincerity Sinclair said he felt bad about them leaving so soon. Then when this byplay had reached its finale the Jaguar moved slowly away. At last he was rid of them.

Through Bridge of Allan to the village of Causeway-head, just beyond. They drove on, to the open road. And it was then they saw the stationary limousine, a uniformed chauffeur peering under the bonnet.

As he was evidently having trouble Peter pulled up.

'Can I give you a hand?'

The man glanced towards his passengers, hunched up in the back of the car, then lowered the bonnet hurriedly.

'No, thank you, sir. It's all right now.'

Peter drove on, a tiny groove of thought forming between his eyes. The chauffeur's reply had been prompted by his passenger. Clearly he had not wished to be recognised, but the brief glimpse Peter had obtained had been enough.

He wondered what had brought the Prime Minister to that part of Scotland.

Part Two

1

1

The man in possession would not have been an inapt description of the under-sized, hatched-faced man whom Peter found reclining luxuriously in the best arm-chair in his Jermyn Street flat. This rather scruffy intruder was smoking one of Peter's cigars and judging from the partly empty whisky bottle at his elbow and his mellowed and contented expression, it seemed that he would have been quite happy if this period of waiting had been indefinitely prolonged.

As it was, it was rudely shattered by Gayleigh's appearance. Fortunately, perhaps. For he was still able to stand, which he did albeit unsteadily.

'Wotcher, guv'ner!' He eyed the whisky bottle, then gazed with owlish intensity at the glowing tip of his cigar. 'Jest helped meself like. Knew yer wouldn't mind.'

'Not at all,' said Peter dryly. 'Now sit down before you fall down.'

He was not surprised to find him there. He had been expecting him before he had met Carver in the hall, his man informing him with ill-concealed disapproval that: 'The person by the name of Orne is waiting, sir.' Carver the sedate automaton: Albert Orne, petty thief and opportunist. Both these men, dissimilar in most respects would have given their all for Peter Gayleigh.

As Diana had found, he affected the privileged few who worked for him in that way. There was something in his vital personality that bound his satellites to him with enduring loyalties. It was partly the buccaneering recklessness in those cool blue eyes; partly his inherent capacity for overcoming any obstacle; but in the main that indefinable attribute of the born leader.

Albert sank back into the chair, suddenly conscious that he was not feeling at his best.

'I ain't tight, guvner,' he said very earnestly. 'Corse I've had a few, but I know jest what I'm doin'.'

'I don't doubt it,' Peter told him, and to the little man's dismay moved the whisky bottle out of reach. 'When did you get my wire?'

'Ternight, guv, soon as I got 'ome. I came round here right away.'

Peter had sent the telegram from Stirling, and as Diana had known nothing of Albert's activities had given her a brief explanation.

'While you and I have been darting hither and thither in bonny Scotland, Albert has been keeping tabs on Shirley Quentin. You remember she was expected back in town on the day we went north.'

Diana had cocked her blonde head on one side, regarding him speculatively.

'That's why you left her to her own devices?'

'Precisely.'

'H'm. So that explains it — knowing you I was surprised you didn't investigate the feminine angle of this business first.'

'Only, my sweet, because I fancy it's going to be a wee bit difficult to get this girl to talk.'

They had not hurried unduly during the journey south, since business with pleasure was one of his precepts. Then realising this might also apply to Orne, he had left Diana at her London flat and returned to his own, thereby thwarting Albert's rising hopes of making a night of it.

'Well?' he prompted. 'Let's hear what you've got.'

'I ain't got nothin' today, guv. This Quentin chick ain't left her flat in Earl's Court — leastways not so far as I know. Y'see there's a back door and since I can't cover both front and back, she might have slipped out that way.' He rubbed his thin chin ruminatively. 'It's queer her staying indoors terday. Before that she'd been gettin' around quite a bit.'

Peter sprayed cigarette smoke over his lower lip, frowning slightly. This could mean she had realised Orne was keeping an eye on her. Either that or — Had Sinclair warned her? His incipient frown deepened.

'Are you sure she's still there? She could have packed a bag and gone. You'd better find out in the morning and ring me. Does she live alone?'

No, she had a maid, he was told.

'She's cost me a packet, guv — tailin' her around. Taxis all the time. I got my expenses 'ere,' he added hopefully, fumbling in his pocket. He produced a battered pocket book, opening it.

Peter gave one glance at the well filled page before handing it back.

'It must have taken you quite a time to fake that,' he remarked. 'Here's a fiver. You're not as drunk as I thought you were.' And as Albert pocketed it quickly: 'Where did this Quentin girl go?'

'Shoppin' mostly, guv. Cor blimey, I bin in more shops than a dress salesman! Then she took in a show one night, by herself.'

'Are you telling me she met nobody at all?'

'Not until yesterday she didn't.' He paused, drawing knowingly at his cigar. He had reached the peak point of his report which must be conveyed with due effort.

'Then she went to the *Green Mask*

— twice!' he said.

In the act of mixing himself a drink, Peter looked up sharply. The *Green Mask* was in Frith Street, Soho. Separate cubicles, discreet waiters, subdued lighting. It catered for the wealthier flotsam and jetsam of London's night life. It managed to be expensive without being select.

'She 'ad lunch there with one bloke,' Albert went on, 'and dinner with another. Corse I 'ad to stay outside, but I had a word with the doorman. Me and Mike did a stretch at Pentonville,' he explained. 'It kind of forges a bond. Same as the old school tie. Well, Mike told me the Quentin chick had bin there reg'lar with these geezers. In fact there used to be three of 'em. There was another bloke called Stroud.

Peter's eyebrows lowered fractionally.

'You got the names of the other two?'

'Sure. One of 'em is called Maynard — Humphrey Maynard. The other is a furriner. Osvald Eidervik. Mike had heard the girl call 'em by their first names. That's how I got 'em.'

'I'd like a description of these two, Albert.'

'Okay. Maynard is dark, and abart your height. But he stoops a lot and wears glasses. Looks like he'd done a lot of book reading. Peaky-faced, weedy sort of bloke.'

'And the Norwegian?'

'Yer mean Eidervik? He's blond and beefy. Fills his clothes same as if he was poured into 'em. He could have a yen for this Shirley chick the way Mike said he looked at her. She always met these two blokes at different times — never together, he said. This Eidervik looks pretty tough, but Maynard don't. I reckon a good wind would blow him over. He's English. I 'eard him speak to Mike as he left the joint alone after seeing the girl. His voice reminded me of yourn.'

'H'm.' Peter sampled his drink reflectively. 'Let's see if we can find where they live.' He crossed to the telephone directory, flicking over the pages. 'Here we are,' he said presently: 'Maynard Humphrey, 10, Ferndale Crescent, Hampstead.' He made a note of the phone number, then resumed his search. But this time unsuccessfully. Eidervik's name was not listed.

Did these two men know each other? In all probability they did since they had both met the girl at the *Green Mask*, though never together. And she had made appointments with them soon after Sinclair had spoken on the scrambler telephone to Gundersen. Before that she had been visiting friends in Devon, Herrington had said. But had she? She could have made one of her periodic visits to Scotland — to Castle Dreich.

If so it could be assumed that she had seen Alan Sinclair there. Which suggested that Sinclair also knew Maynard and Eidervik, and that this footloose girl was acting as a go between.

'All right, Albert,' he said. 'I think we're progressing. Now you'd better get along and sleep off my whisky. Then back on the job tomorrow.'

In Albert's present condition a taxi was definitely indicated. Peter phoned for one, and in due course saw him into it. As he returned to his flat he was quite unaware that he had been observed by the man who had shot Vincent Stroud.

Orne's unwanted interest in Shirley Quentin had been noted much earlier. He had been followed by the heavy-jowled man now sitting in a saloon car farther up Jermyn Street. He was smoking a cigarette, holding it between thick, spatulate fingers, his gross, Teutonic features under his greying blond hair quite expressionless.

The Herr Doktor Ulrich von Shroeder was considering how he would deal with this unexpected complication.

2

The curtains were still drawn, but as Peter shrugged himself into wakefulness he realised that the phone in the lounge was ringing. A moment later it stopped, Carver entering soon afterwards to advise him, in a tone of infinite disparagement, that Mr. Orne was calling.

'I thought I'd give you a tinkle, guv,' Albert said. 'I bin on the job since six this mornin'. Never felt better in me perishing life. I reckon that whisky of yourn is a real tonic. Maybe I need whisky just like some folk need vitamins.'

'An absorbing thought, I agree,' said Peter. 'Any fresh developments?'

'No, guv. But I seen both her and the maid movin' abart. So she ain't checked out yet.'

'Thanks, Albert,' Shirley Quentin, it seemed, was an early riser. 'Keep in touch.'

He hung up, found her number in the directory, and dialled it. No time like the present, he thought.

'Hullo?' It was a woman's voice.

'Is that Miss Quentin?'

'No, this is Miss Quentin's maid speaking. Who is that, please?'

'My name is Gayleigh,' he said very deliberately. 'Peter Gayleigh,' he added, in case there should be any misconception.

There was a short pause. Then:

'I'm sorry, sir, Miss Quentin left early this morning for the country. I'm afraid she won't be back for several days.'

'Is that so?' he said. 'How very

unfortunate. I was looking forward to seeing her. Will you tell Miss Quentin that? No not just yet — it will do when she moves from your elbow.'

He hung up with a sardonic smile. He thought it was a pity he couldn't observe the effect on Miss Quentin, but the seed had been sown. Now it must be given time to germinate. His name seemed to be in bad odour with this girl he had never met. Could it have been Sinclair who had warned her against him? That possibility, he decided, was far from remote.

Later in the day he heard further from Albert — nothing of any consequence. Miss Quentin had visited a hairdresser in the morning, and done some shopping. In the afternoon she had taken in a matineé. She had not gone out at all in the evening most of which Peter had spent in the vicinity of Humphrey Maynard's house in Hampstead.

It was almost eight o'clock when he returned to Jermyn Street, to be advised by his tenacious ally that Shirley Quentin was still at her flat.

'Don't look as if she's goin' out again, guv.'

'She will, Albert. Oh yes, I think so,' he added, with what might have been prescience. 'But from now on I propose to take care of her myself. So you can cut along home, chum. I'll ring you tomorrow.'

He pressed down the receiver-rest, then dialled her number again.

'Hullo?' It was the maid.

'Mr. Gayleigh calling. If it wouldn't be too much trouble do you think I might have the pleasure of speaking to Miss Quentin now?'

As before there was a pause, rather shorter this time. When the response came it was undeniably cold.

'Miss Quentin is not at home, sir. As I told you this morning — '

'Please!' he interpolated with gentle reproach. 'Must you labour the point? Try the other side of the record. It's rendered by the Quentin trio — which includes Maynard and Eidervik. It used to be a quartet, I believe, but Stroud couldn't quite make the grade. There will now be

106

an interval while you inform Miss Quentin of that. I'll ring again later.'

He severed the connection — then dialled the number again with undiminished optimism. At this point no time must be wasted, otherwise the elusive Shirley would certainly get busy on her own account. The ringing note told him the phone was not being used again as yet, and he waited nonchalantly until he heard the maid's familiar inquiry.

'I want to speak to Miss Quentin.' All the mockery had gone from his voice now, as he spoke through his handkerchief spread over the mouthpiece, his tone carrying impatient irritability. 'This is Mr. Maynard.'

There was a pause. Then another feminine voice said: 'The old lady — '

' — with a bustle,' he returned promptly.

'Shirley here.' Her tone was strained. 'I was just going to ring you, Humphrey.'

Peter said: 'What's that. I can hardly hear you.'

Apparently she was having the same difficulty. It was mutually agreed that they had got a bad line. Then she repeated: 'I was just going to ring you.'

'Oh?' He put a wealth of significance into the word.

'About a man called Gayleigh — Peter Gayleigh.'

'Gayleigh!' He spoke with chagrin. 'I might have guessed it. So he phoned you, too!'

'You mean — ?'

'Yes. That man is dangerous. What did he say to you?'

She told him. She wasn't word perfect, probably because the maid had abridged his remarks. But if they had lost some of their insolence they had acquired a gratifying menace. Peter examined his fingernails and tried to judge this version impartially. He wasn't biased. He had to admit it was an improvement.

'Yes, much the same as he said to me, Shirley.'

'And I was right about what I told you yesterday,' she went on anxiously.

She paused, obviously waiting for his comment. What the devil had she told Maynard? Careful, my lad!

'Are you sure?' he said, tossing the ball back.

'Absolutely certain. He's gone now, but he was outside my flat all day. Then, almost immediately after he'd gone I got another of these phone calls.'

'I see. You think he was working for Gayleigh?'

'Yes, I do, Humphrey. It couldn't have been one of — the others.'

The others? He digested this, his hesitation evidently giving her the impression that he hadn't grasped her point.

'Don't you *see*?' she went on impatiently. 'Gayleigh mentioned all three of us — and Stroud! He knows we're working together although you've never met Osvald and, don't forget, I've been away in Scotland. Gayleigh was in Scotland, too, he only returned yesterday. So when I met you at — in Soho he couldn't have followed me. But this other man could, I wish I'd spotted him sooner.'

'So do I,' Peter said with appropriate anxiety. 'This is serious, Shirley. Gayleigh is a notorious character, an insolent buccaneer. But we can't discuss this over the phone.'

'No . . . '

'Could you come over to my place right away?'

He noticed her hesitation, somewhat puzzled, until she said: 'Well — It's against instructions, you know. We're not supposed to call on each other.'

'Of course not,' he said swiftly. 'But it can't matter just this once. Besides, I haven't booked a table at our usual place tonight. And you do realise we must talk this over as soon as possible. Don't wait to phone Osvald,' he added advisedly. 'You can tell him later, after we've decided what to do.'

'Yes . . . Very well I'll come.'

'I'll be waiting for you,' he said, and meant it. 'Good-bye.'

He put the phone daintily back on its stand, eyeing it speculatively for a few moments with the satisfaction of a job well done. Then he went to his car parked in readiness outside.

He must get to Hampstead before she arrived.

2

1

There were those who said that Peter Gayleigh never made a false move when pursuing his favourite occupation — that of intruding where he was not wanted. It was, of course, untrue, as he would have admitted with becoming modesty. Often there had been difficulties, and he knew his limitations. More specifically, he knew that to force his way into Humphrey Maynard's house like a common thief would not have been easy. Both the front and back doors were very substantial and, as he had observed earlier that evening, the windows were equipped with shutters which would probably be drawn after dark.

The house itself stood in about an acre of ground, less than a quarter of a mile from Hampstead Heath. It was approached from the front by a short circular drive, a tall privet hedge shielding the lower windows. A path led round to the back, the garden, mostly lawn, flanked by more tall hedges leading up to a high wall, and a tradesman's gate.

Maynard, he had surmised from Orne's description, was a studious type. And since he was connected with Gundersen that could mean he was some kind of boffin. But whatever he was, it was clear that by accident or design he had surrounded himself with privacy.

He parked the Jaguar in a road bordering the Heath, walking the rest of the way to his appointment. Even if the man was not at home, the meeting with the girl would not lack piquency, though he hoped that Maynard would be there to share in the general bonhomie.

It was a dark, cloudy night which suited his purpose admirably. As he slipped into the short drive he could barely distinguish the outline of the house from the starless sky. No lights showed in any of the windows, the shutters had been drawn. His immediate object was a laurel bush standing only a few feet away from the steps leading to the front door. He moved stealthily up to it, and behind it, taking advantage of its cover.

He had to wait nearly ten minutes before Shirley Quentin arrived. Presumably she had taken a taxi, but had dismissed it before reaching the house, for she came on foot. He heard her turn into the drive. She was walking quickly, passing very close to him as she mounted the steps and rang the front door bell. All he could see in the darkness was that she was fairly tall and slim.

The bell brought no response at first. With an impatience he could well understand she rang again, his heart rejoicing as he heard the sound of bolts being withdrawn. Then a widening shaft of light from the hall spilled over the steps, presenting him with a much better view of her. A firm chin and a classical profile, a boyish figure and Ballito clad legs which were far from boyish. She was not wearing a hat, her silky blonde hair reminding him of Diana's. She was, he thought, quite lovely.

But it was merely a fleeting thought, for by now a tall, weedy man, evidently Maynard, had appeared at the door.

'Why, Shirley!' he exclaimed. Then sharply. 'What are you doing here?'

'What am I doing here? Why — ' She broke off staring at him blankly. In a brief silence that ensued Peter could almost see her mind working.

'Humphrey!' Anxiety had overcome surprise.

'What's the matter? Is something wrong? Surely you know we had strict instructions — '

'So you didn't phone me!'

'Phone you. Of course not. What — ?'

'Let me in. Quickly!' she said, starting forward.

It was Gayleigh's cue. One lithe effortless leap carried him on to the steps; another, equally swift, beyond the front door. And as she had not got that far he accelerated her progress with the flat of his hand, pressing it between her shoulders and pushing hard as he came. Her entrance lacked elegance, but that was unavoidable. Just two seconds after springing into action he was in the house, kicking the door shut with his heel.

The girl was still careering along the hall when Maynard seemed to realise what was happening. His hand went to his jacket pocket, but by Gayleigh's standards he was a little slow in producing a snub-nosed automatic.

Steel-like fingers gripped his arm above the elbow. At the same moment a bony wrist was twisted. The gun was slipping from Maynard's fingers when it found a new home in Gayleigh's palm.

'Better this way, chum. Neither of us want to get hurt.'

His gaze flashed towards the girl farther up the hall. She had swung round now, clutching her handbag, much too hopefully.

'I wouldn't open it,' he said. 'It might be safer if you gave it to me.'

She made no move to obey, her lips tightly compressed.

'If you want it, come and get it.'

Peter sighed tolerantly. 'Whenever I wrestle with a lady I prefer to be alone. We might try it sometime, but not now.'

She had eyes like tropical skies in which lightning seemed to be crackling. Definitely a girl who showed her emotions.

'The impertinent Mr. Gayleigh, of course,' she snapped.

'In person.' He paid tribute to this deduction with an ironical inclination of his head. 'And this gentleman, who seems to have outgrown his strength, is, I take it Mr. Humphrey Maynard.'

That lanky individual was now looking as if he had been pecked by an extremely obnoxious and presumptuous bird.

'Perhaps,' he said, 'you will condescend to explain why you have forced your way into my house and why you persist in behaving in this outrageous manner?'

Faced with this rebuke it must be admitted that Peter blinked a little. For he had always been under the impression that such phraseology had gone out with side whiskers and pantaloons. Apparently not. You could always learn.

'Come, come, Humphrey!' he said. 'Let's not be haughty. That's Miss Quentin's prerogative. We mustn't deprive her of it, must we?'

Maynard glowered at him, massaging his bruised wrist.

'I've heard about you — ' he was beginning again, somewhat plaintively, when the girl cut him short.

'All right, Humphrey. Let me talk to him.' Her tone was much more incisive. And as she switched her gaze: 'Mr. Maynard is not accustomed to dealing with men like you. He happens to be a gentleman.'

'Indeed! Could he also be a biologist?'

The stormy blue eyes flickered fractionally. 'Never mind that. What do you want with us?'

'Since you press the point,' he said, 'I'll tell you. I came to get some information, and I've no intention of leaving until I get it. To put it another way, I'd like to know what's going on. In Scotland I gave your fiancé every opportunity to open his heart to me, but alas! I found him very reticent.'

'You mean you went there to spy on him,' she retorted. 'A man who was your friend.' She was breathing heavily through her nose. 'How contemptible can you get!'

'That's a harsh word, Shirley. But it depends what you mean by contemptible. I see nothing wrong in trying to discover why your pal Stroud was murdered. Such a pity! He seemed to know a great deal about you.'

A thrust which brought a slight quiver to her lips, some of the tenseness vanishing from her expression.

'Oh, why can't you mind your own business?' she said bitterly.

'Regrettably, perhaps, it has never been a habit of mine.'

'We're not criminals, if that's what you think.'

'No, frankly I don't. I've already come to the conclusion that 'the others' you mentioned over the phone are the villains of the piece. Incidentally, I thought I saw one of that tribe in Scotland. He followed your Alan, then took pot shots at him in his spare time. He didn't have much more spare time, as you probably know.'

But as he saw them exchange sharp, puzzled glances, he realised they didn't know. Shirley and her far from stalwart cohort were not told everything, apparently.

'You mean you *haven't* been told?' he resumed, with elaborate surprise. 'I really think you should be. So suppose we let our hair down and have a heart to heart talk.'

Neither of them said anything immediately, the girl still staring at him resentfully, Maynard seemingly fascinated by the gun that covered him. But despite his ineffectual manner he proved that he was a realist.

'Perhaps that would be just as well,' he said stiffly. 'You appear to have been very busy.'

Peter shrugged. 'Since this promises to be a lengthy discussion I propose we move to somewhere more comfortable. I had a room and some chairs in mind.'

'I was about to suggest that,' was the distant reply. 'If you will follow me — '

He turned away walking to a door near the end of the hall, Peter moving up behind him, barely pausing as he drew level with the girl. His hand shot out. A split second later he had her handbag.

'Sorry, honey,' he said blandly. 'But you told me to come and get it. Remember?'

She was staring at him furiously when he opened it. Inside was a small .22 pistol.

'Tch! Tch! And I thought you were a lady. Shame on you, Shirley! Could it be that you hoped to use this on me?'

Without deigning to reply she followed Maynard to the room door, her chin held high. The door was ajar, a slip mat just outside, the room itself being in semi-gloom, illuminated only by the light from the hall. It was evidently a library-cum-study, a fat tome lying open on a desk, testifying to Maynard's scholarly pursuits.

'All right, Humphrey.' The man had paused outside the doorway. 'Let's go in. You two first!'

Maynard went in, switching on the light, the girl sidling after him without taking her eyes from Peter's face. Unprepared for any unusual eventuality at that moment, he didn't notice that both of them had avoided stepping on the slip mat.

It was a mistake — for as he followed

them in it happened!

He had one foot on the mat, his head just inside the door when something crashed down from the lintel above. The blow caught him on the back of his skull, sending him reeling to his knees. Flashes of blinding light split up into fragments and died behind a veil of deepening blackness. Then as oblivion claimed him the gun was wrenched from his grasp.

2

Humphrey Maynard stepped back, avoiding Gayleigh's limp body as it slumped to the carpet. There was a tense unnatural silence broken by the girl's anxious voice.

'I hope he isn't — ?'

'No, it isn't heavy enough to kill him.' But he didn't seem all that sure, neither of them looking like hardened conspirators.

As he put his gun back in his jacket pocket she bent down stretching out a tentative hand to feel Gayleigh's pulse. Then satisfied that he was still alive, she turned her head towards the door.

A heavy metal bar was now dangling there only a few inches above the slip mat. The bar was supported by two wires running up to small pulleys in the lintel.

'A rather crude contraption, I'm afraid,' Maynard said. 'But as I told you I fitted it up myself. I don't profess to be a handy man. But as this is the room where I keep the papers you entrust to me — '

'I wonder how much he knows?' she said, interrupting him as she stared down at their victim, retrieving her handbag from the floor.

'Very little I should imagine. These kind of men rely mainly on bluff, I believe.'

She nodded, very unhappily. 'I wish to heaven I hadn't come here. But over the phone his voice sounded just like yours. Besides, he used our code words.'

'He did?' All his previous agitation returned as he blinked at her.

'And that isn't all he knows, Humphrey. He mentioned Osvald's name, as well as yours and Alan's. He knows we're all working together.'

Maynard blinked again. 'Confound the man,' he said fretfully. And with undeniable logic: 'We can well do without this sort of thing.'

'You can say that again,' she retorted, biting her lip. 'Somehow we've got to stop him from interfering.'

'Yes.'

'What are we going to do with him. We can't just leave him here?'

There was a short silence, Maynard massaging his thin chin.

'To my mind there is only one way to deal with this situation,' he said, in his precise way. 'As you rightly say, he must be prevented from making a further nuisance of himself. He has behaved like a common law breaker, forcing his way into my house and threatening me with a gun. That being so, I propose to let the police take care of him.'

These were the first words Peter heard as returning consciousness carried him back to reality. And as he remained with his eyes closed, fighting down the hammer beat in his head, he wondered if he had heard correctly. For there were a great many other things Maynard might have done, things which the ungodly had not hesitated to do, often with malicious satisfaction when the dice had fallen their way. But not this man. He was a gentleman. He was simply going to call the police.

Such righteousness was, no doubt, commendable, though if the boot had been on the other foot Peter would never have considered such a solution. He didn't consider it now, squinting up at Mr. Maynard through half-closed eyes. Almost he could feel sorry for him. When it came to rough stuff he was so obviously out of his depth.

'He may recover consciousness at any moment,' he was saying. 'There is no necessity for you to remain, Shirley. You can leave this to me.'

The girl hesitated, not without good cause, Peter thought.

'All right,' she said, doubtfully. 'I suppose there's no reason why both of us should get mixed up with the police.'

'No, that is exactly what I was thinking.'

Still she hesitated. 'You will be careful, Humphrey. They'll ask you an awful lot of question you know.'

'I am aware of that,' he said with a conspicuous lack of enthusiasm. 'But I fancy my reputation will stand me in good stead, whereas this man is a notorious adventurer. You had better leave by the back way. You'll find the door bolted.' He eyed their victim, who showed no signs of coming round. 'On second thoughts I'd better come with you to make it secure again after you've gone. It won't take a minute.'

'Very well. You must phone me as soon as you can, Humphrey.'

'Yes, of course.'

And they walked past him, stepping over the dangling bludgeon into the hall. Two very optimistic people, Peter thought, though they had hardly given him that impression. As their footsteps receded he got quietly, if somewhat dizzily, to his feet. He heard the back door bolts being withdrawn, followed by a few muffled words of farewell. Then the sound of the bolts again and

Maynard returning.

He would shortly be doing quite a lot of talking — but not over the phone.

Peter waited behind the open door, darting round it and grabbing him before he had time to realise that all was not as it should be.

'Mind the step, Humphrey,' he said, lifting him bodily over his home-made contraption. 'We don't want any more accidents, do we?'

He set him down in the room, the struggle that ensued extremely brief. Mr. Maynard was no in-fighter. With almost effortless ease he was deprived of his gun again, Peter tossing it away across the room.

'Something tells me we shan't need that,' he said, releasing him. 'Now we can be really matey.'

Maynard straightened his tie, glaring at him.

'I should have known better,' he breathed bitterly.

Peter shrugged. 'All of us make mistakes, Humphrey. I made mine, now you've made yours. But you'll be making another unless you become more amenable. Believe me I can turn quite nasty. Now, at the risk of repeating myself you know what I want.'

'You may do what you please,' Maynard said valiantly. 'I shall say nothing.'

'To proceed,' said Peter, ignoring this. 'We'll come to your Scottish contingent later, taking in Sinclair, Gundersen, and your unfortunate pal Stroud *en passant*. We'll start with you and Miss Quentin, and the rest of the London clique. Apart from Eidervik how many more of you are playing this game?'

This brought no reply. Maynard simply stood there giving a further impression of a man whose lips were permanently sealed.

Peter gripped his arm, pushing him towards his desk.

'If you'll stop behaving like a martyr,' he said, 'it will save both of us a lot of time. This, I imagine, is the room where you keep your deepest secrets. I also presume they will not be revealed without the help of your keys. So you'd better hand 'em over, and pretty damned quick. Because if you don't — '

Suddenly he stiffened, his eyes darting towards the door.

Footsteps! Very faint but unmistakable. Someone was moving furtively in the hall.

A second later Maynard heard it too, his resolute, tight-lipped expression crumbling.

'The front door!' he exclaimed, his voice hoarse with agitation. 'You didn't lock it!'

It was a most inopportune outburst, for immediately there was a scurrying sound. The front door, which must have been left ajar, closed with a loud bang. Then Maynard swung round with frantic haste, about to dash out into the hall. He had taken one stride in that direction when Gayleigh shot out an arm, yanking him back.

'Not so fast, brother! Why the hell can't you talk at the right time?'

'But you don't understand — '

'Get out of my way, you fool!'

He thrust him aside, and bounded into

the hall, dashing towards the front door. He opened it smartly, peering out into the garden, now partly illuminated by the light spilling out behind him. He could see as far as the privet hedge, but no one was in sight. The delay in dealing with Maynard had evidently been enough for this prowler. He could easily have slipped away round the back. He could have done, unless —

The laurel bush near the foot of the steps! Since the intruder couldn't have got far, possibly — And now in the stillness of the night he thought he could detect the faint sound of breathing coming from behind it. But he couldn't be sure because he could also hear Maynard coming along the hall.

He could have done without him at that moment, and very unwisely disregarded him. For as he leaned farther out of the door, scrutinising the bush intently, he was suddenly pushed violently forward, and as he staggered down the steps the door was slammed behind him. He was still trying vainly to recover his balance when he heard the lock snap into place, followed by the distinctive thud of a bolt.

Mr. Humphrey Maynard had seen his chance and taken it.

3

As his hands and knees made forcible contact with the gravelled drive the imprecations Peter Gayleigh uttered did nothing to lessen his chagrin. The prospect of re-entering the house now seemed to be remote. But he was not given time to consider the possibilities, or even to dwell on his next move. For with startling suddeness, his mind was made up for him.

A bullet whipped past his ankles boring a neat hole in his trousers' leg. There was no loud report, only a sound as if a cushion had been struck with a cane, before the bullet ploughed into the gravel. A silencer had been used, the shot coming from the direction of the laurel bush.

Gayleigh realised both these things as

he stiffened. He was too far away from the bush, which had once served his own purpose, to make a dive towards it. Before he could reach it to grapple with this marksman he would certainly have taken another bullet. But if he stayed where he was devoid of any cover his prospects were decidely bleak. He had to move, and quick.

The only spot that offered any shelter was the other side of the steps. He leapt in that direction, another bullet whistling past him before he could reach this temporary haven. He was lucky to have made it, he thought grimly, as he flung himself down behind the stonework. Quite evidently this gunman meant business, and with belated yearning he thought of Maynard's gun which he had tossed so nonchalantly aside. He could have done with it now.

The gunman had seen his attempt at evasion and had only to come and get him.

Even so, nothing happened for more than a minute. It was rather puzzling, until it occurred to him that his assailant probably thought he was armed. For this must be the eavesdropper, and from what he had overheard in the hall he might have come to that conclusion.

Whether he had or not he was being very canny.

Peter risked a glance over the top of the steps. He could see the outline of the bush, but no indication of any lurking figure there. Which was hardly surprising, he realised a moment later, as a third bullet smashed against the wall above him, coming from an entirely different angle. From the darkness farther along the opposite side of the drive. The man had improved his position, still cautious, but facing him almost directly now.

Taking advantage of the soft earth of an empty flowerbed bordering the wall, Peter moved another couple of yards away from the steps. If he could reach the path round to the back of the house . . .

Another bullet checked him, narrowly missing his shoulder.

He froze again, swallowing heavily, the cool night air fanning the cold perspiration on his forehead. Fate seemed to be conspiring against him, for since his forceful ejection from the house nobody had passed along the quiet street beyond the hedge. He felt as much alone as a trapper beset by a wolf in the enveloping darkness.

Another minute passed that seemed to stretch into eternity. There were no more shots, no sound of any movement. Yet he sensed his invisible assailant was still there, waiting with calculating determination.

The minute lengthened into two. Still no discernible sound, only agonising suspense. Surely by now the man must have realised he was unarmed? But apparently not. Was he creeping closer to get a better aim? The uncertainty twanged at Gayleigh's nerves as he strove vainly to pierce the darkness. The silence and the waiting was becoming intolerable.

Very cautiously he began to move again, edging inch by inch along the flower-bed, his back flattened against the dark wall, praying that he would appear to be part of it. The side path was still several yards away, beyond a shuttered window of the house.

He reached the window, glided like a phantom past it without attracting any further response from his invisible adversary. He had almost begun to wonder if the man had gone when another bullet told him he hadn't. But this time it went very wide, ricochetting from the wall nearer the front door, at the spot where he had been standing before. Evidently the gunman thought he hadn't moved from there, which was some consolation. Even so, he was unable to assess the direction from which the shot came.

The opening to the side path was almost in sight now, and as he resumed his slow, silent progress over the soft earth it came into view. Only another couple of yards more. With renewed hope he edged closer . . . still closer. Yes, he had made it! He gripped the brickwork with his sweating palm and darted round on to the path.

A moment later his nerves quivered afresh as a hand gripped his arm.

3

1

His immediate thought was that it had all been in vain, except that now he had at least come to grips with his devilish assailant. At the same time it struck him that it was surprising he had been given this opportunity, until a voice said: 'This way. Round the back. Quickly!'

It was a woman's voice. Not Shirley Quentin's. He had never heard it before. Already she was pulling at his arm urging him on, though he needed no inducement. If she had been a witch born of the night he wouldn't have cared. She moved ahead of him, a dark, fleeting figure, making practically no sound as he followed her into the back garden and across the lawn to the gate. It was outlined by the pale light from a street lamp in the narrow thoroughfare beyond, and he saw that it was partly open.

Presumably she must have come that way after Shirley Quentin had left.

They reached it and darted through, hurrying away along the street. By now he had seen that she was wearing a navy blue anorak, the hood hiding most of her face, a black skirt, and a pair of black sneakers.

She was half-running half-walking ahead of him and they were well clear of the house before she slowed down.

'You're Peter Gayleigh, aren't you?' she said, rather breathlessly.

'Yes.'

'I thought you must be.' She didn't say why she thought so. And as she glanced back over her shoulder: 'I think we've given him the slip.'

'Yes, it looks that way.'

'I daresay you're wondering who I am?'

'That's putting it mildly.'

'I know where you parked your car,' she said, increasing her pace. 'Come on! I've a lot to tell you, but we can't talk yet.'

She sounded very pleased with herself, her eyes shining with accomplishment. In the indeterminate light they appeared to be a greenish-violet, the thick, silky lashes very pronounced. Her rather pointed chin gave her an impish appearance, accentuated by the knowing tilt of her mouth. She was in her early twenties, he judged.

As they walked on in silence he kept eyeing her sideways, thinking that her face was vaguely familiar. Where had he seen it before? And what had she been doing outside Maynard's house, sneaking about there?

His car was still standing where he had left it, and after another glance along the way they had come he unlocked the doors and motioned her in. He brought the engine to life and drove for about half a mile in the direction of Golders Green, before pulling up.

'You're sure we haven't been followed,' she said.

'Quite sure.' He produced his cigarette-case proferring it as she removed the hood of her anorak. If her hair had matched her eyebrows it would have been black. Actually it was a rich chestnut, slightly disarranged. As she turned towards him, a truant strand slid caressingly over her check. She looked very feminine and even less mature.

'Thanks,' she said, 'I can do with one!'

He took one himself and snapped his lighter into flame, studying her face more closely as he lit both cigarettes.

'You know, I've a feeling I've seen you somewhere before,' he said. 'But I can't just remember — '

'In the Society magazines perhaps. I'm Corinne Raeburn.'

She proclaimed it with a defiant tilt of her chin, and as though it should mean something.

It did. Lord Bromley's daughter! In her less abandoned moments she had often found time to be photographed, usually with some wealthy playboy she had picked up, or with another woman's husband.

'Ah yes!' he said. 'God's gift to the photographers.'

'Perhaps.' Her greenish eyes narrowed slightly. 'But don't forget I've been a godsend to you. If I hadn't happened along tonight — '

'Just how did you happen along?' he interrupted gently. 'I'd be interested to hear.'

The tip of her cigarette described an arc, glowing brightly as she drew at it, before letting it fall to her knee again.

'Presently. There's a time and place for everything. I knew a French count once who thought he'd found both until I disillusioned him. I was very young then, fresh from finishing school, and oh so very, very difficult. Poor man, I feel sorry for him now. The others had much more luck. Oh yes, I'm not denying I've slept around.' The full, sensuous lips tilted reminiscently. 'But I've never met a man like you. Like me you've a reputation for doing just what you want to do. I've been thinking we're well matched.'

Peter said dryly: 'Is that a suggestion, or a firm proposition?'

'You can take it either way. Since we've so much to talk about we could go to my apartment.'

'I suppose we could,' he said, very conscious of her insinuating nearness and the subtlety of expensive perfume. 'Or we could go somewhere for a bite to eat. More neutral ground, as it were.'

'I see.' She gave him a very arch look.

'You like to take your time.'

'On the contrary. I'd just like to hear why you go prowling about in other people's gardens at night.'

'I don't make a habit of it,' she assured him, with a tiny smile. 'But all that can wait. Where are you going to take me?'

'Well, we could try the *Green Mask*.'

His eyes were on her face, but if the name meant anything to her there was nothing in her reply that suggested he was probing inhibitions.

'The *Green Mask*? I don't know the place. Is it near here?'

'No, in Soho.'

'Then why go all that way?' And she snuggled closer to him lifting his arm and putting it round her shoulders. 'There! Isn't that better?'

Her hair was brushing his cheek, her seductive nearness very enticing. Her profile had all the clean-cut prefection of an ancient Egyptian queen and, he reminded himself, he owed her something. If she wanted it this way . . . His arm had slid down to her slim waist as she raised her head, her lips inviting. He could feel her warm breath on his face, the soft yielding of her body, the pressure of his hand tightening about her.

And it was then his fingers detected something in the pocket of her anorak, something far from yielding and of a chillingly familiar shape. He could feel it through the soft material — a small gun, with a bulb silencer attached to the barrel.

2

In that instant of electric awareness he recalled several things that had puzzled him. Though his assailant had seemed to be in deadly earnest, none of the bullets had found their mark. Yet he, himself, had been in full view when the first shot had sent him diving for cover. Then, instead of coming closer, this supposed gunman had glided farther away, firing more shots while slowly creeping round in what could have been a semi-circle. And while his prey was sweating it out this sniper could have reached the side passage.

Waiting there! Nicely in position to put the final touches to the charade.

He knew now beyond a shadow of doubt that it had been so.

What fun she must have had! What a perverted sense of humour, enjoying his predicament while deliberately firing wide. Oh yes, deliberately, for she had the reputation of being an excellent shot — the notorious Corinne Raeburn who would do anything for a fresh experience.

But apart from her sadistic inclinations she must have had some reason for making his acquaintance. And since he had yet to learn what it was, and because he was used to dealing with abnormal situations, his cool blue eyes betrayed no indication of his deeper feelings.

'What are you waiting for?' she whispered, with nauseating urgency, her hands coming up to his cheeks caressingly.

'Well, strange as it may seem,' he said, 'I'm rather old fashioned in some ways. I don't like being rushed. So we'll wait a little, huh? In the meantime, suppose you tell me more about yourself.'

'You mean about tonight?' She made a little moue of disappointment which in itself was indicative, since he had expected a stronger reaction. So she had still been playing with him. He took both her hands and placed them very firmly back on her lap.

'About tonight,' he emphasised. 'We'll skip the restaurant tête-à-tête, at least for the time being.'

'I like masterful men,' she said, looking at him along her eyes. 'Your way could be my way, Peter. We're two of a kind. I could help you a lot.'

'In that case you might start trying.'

'And stop being a mystery woman?' She shrugged resignedly. 'Okay, let's begin the inquisition. First question?'

Peter drew smoke into his lungs expelling it slowly.

'Every heard of Vincent Stroud?'

'No, he's a new one on me. Should I know him?'

'If you haven't met him you never will. He was one of Sinclair's bright boys.'

All this brought was a puzzled frown. It

might have been assumed but he had no way of telling.

'All right. We'll skip that. What about Humphrey Maynard?'

'I don't know him either — at least not to speak to.' She paused, making quite a business of stubbing out her cigarette. 'As you know, he doesn't keep open house. He's rather — exclusive.'

'So I gathered. And I don't see you as one of Miss Quentin's friends.'

She shook her head, offering no enlightenment, pursing her lips provocatively.

'Then do you mind telling me how you come into this?' He took a deep breath. 'Listen sweetheart, I've had a pretty wearing time. Apart from some misadventure in Maynard's house, I've been cornered by a homicidal lunatic with a gun. I've narrowly escaped with my life. And now I've got tangled up with a girl who murmurs sweet nothings, looks at me with wicked eyes and seems to regard me as a lollypop she's still anxious to lick. I'm tired and impatient. So unless you get down to cases I shall leave you and go home to bed. In short, you can keep your precious secrets.'

She wasn't annoyed. He hadn't thought she would be, since she had gone to such lengths to make his acquaintance. She showed two rows of pearly teeth, raising her head as she laughed softly. 'You're wonderful,' she said. 'Sometime I wish Osvald would insult me. He'd be much less boring.'

So here at last was the tie-up.

'Osvald?' he said, as if he had never heard of him.

'Osvald Eidervik. I've known him a month and it's been a month too long.' She shrugged before going on. 'He's a Norwegian I met at a party. I could see he was looking me over, so I jockeyed him along. He didn't appeal to me all that much, but I was at a loose end at the time. He was persistent, and naturally it ended like this.'

She dipped a hand into a pocket in her skirt producing a key, dangling it, looking at him sideways again.

'That's the open sesame to Osvald's flat in Charles Street. He keeps all the windows locked, and I soon realised he wasn't as obvious as I'd thought. For one thing he always carried a gun and often he seemed to be very much on edge, but when I tackled him about it he put me off. He doesn't know how stubborn I can be.'

She paused, thrusting out her small pointed chin.

'And then — ' said Peter promptingly, wondering if this story was sheer fabrication. On the other hand, with so many chapters of erotic endeavour behind her, she could have met Eidervik this way.

'Then, only a few days ago, he rang me to cancel a luncheon engagement. He said he was feeling off colour.'

'You didn't believe him?'

'Do I look that stupid? I took a taxi to his flat and waited near it. I saw him leave and I followed him to — er — to a restaurant, where he met a girl. He didn't stay there with her long and after they'd left I found out her name was Shirley Quentin. Well, I wasn't standing for that sort of brush off, so I went straight back to his flat and had it out with him. He told me she was a business acquaintance, but I told him he could stuff that. It ended up in a first class row.'

'The — er — restaurant you mentioned was the *Green Mask*, perhaps?' Peter said. She had denied all knowledge of it, but now she shrugged. What was one little lie between friends!

'Well, yes it was,' she admitted imperturbably. 'But when you sprung the name on me suggesting we should go there I didn't want to talk about it just then. I wasn't trying to hide anything. It was simply that — '

'Explanation accepted and understood,' he said. 'Sorry I was not in the mood. Do go on.'

She shot him yet another of her sidelong glances.

'That night I had dinner there with another man. And I saw this Quentin girl again. This time she was with Maynard, though I didn't know his name then — not until I made inquiries. Next I went to Hampstead. I found that he was a biologist, like Eidervik, and when I took a look at his house I saw it was just about as impregnable as Osvald's flat. I began to wonder if all three of them were in some sort of shady business together. On both occasions when I'd seen Quentin she hadn't behaved as if she had a yen for either Eidervik or Maynard.'

'So what did you do then?'

'I went to her flat, but her maid told me she'd gone away, and wouldn't be back for some days. Which I didn't believe for one moment — because there was a shabby little man outside obviously watching the place.'

Peter wondered if there was anyone who *hadn't* seen Orne. It couldn't be said that Albert had proved a great success.

'I saw him there, too, when I went there,' he said. 'I wonder who he was?'

There was no mistaking the mockery in her glance.

'I heard you sometimes employ an ex-thief called Albert Orne. Of course he's never made the headlines like you, but — '

'Touché,' For the first time he smiled. 'Go on.'

'So I realised you might be mixed up in this queer business, and I was quite sure you were when I spotted your car parked near the Heath tonight. That was while I was following this mysterious girl to Maynard's house, after she'd taken a taxi from her flat. I'm pretty observant and once I get my teeth into something I never let go.'

'No, I'm sure you don't.'

'When I reached the house the front door was shut, so I waited for a bit, then went round to the back garden. I was there when I saw the back door open and Quentin hurrying away. I was in two minds whether to follow her again or not. But fortunately I didn't, because not long afterwards I heard the front door slam. Then I heard some other sounds — at first I didn't realise they were made by bullets. But I pretty soon did! The rest you know.'

It was a good story, mostly fiction, he thought grimly, her real motives nicely obscured. He might have believed it but for the gun in her pocket. As it was he doubted very much whether she had followed the other girl. She might have done, but it seemed more probable that she had been seeking a way to get into Maynard's house. And he was damned sure she had finally managed it, sneaking into the hall.

'That key you have,' he said reflectively after a few moments. 'It suggests possibilities.'

'Of course it does. It's the only way you'll get into Eidervik's flat. He has a bureau there he always keeps locked.

'I see — and you'd give a lot to see inside it.'

'Wouldn't you? Mind you, it won't be easy,' she went on. 'It's very securely locked. It will need more than skeleton keys to open it, but to a person of your experience it should be possible.'

Peter didn't doubt it. In his less regenerate days there had been few safes that could defy him. A bureau would be child's play, but as he pointed out, Eidervik was liable to object very strongly if he was at home.

'He may not be,' she said. 'But if he is I could phone him. After the row we had I walked out on him, though he rang me this morning trying to smooth it over and make another date. I could pretend I'd had second thoughts, and arrange to meet him somewhere. He's pretty keen on me, and as I'm often late, I'm sure he'd wait for quite a time for me to show up. You could be in Charles Street when he left his flat.'

'With the key.'

'Oh no! I'll keep the key. We'll go together.'

She waited for his comment. Instead he drew the last prospect of sustenance from his cigarette and disposed of it, his lips pursed.

'Well, what do you say?' she urged.

He could have said a great deal, the gun in her pocket colouring his thoughts again. Was she just using him for her own ends, or was she more chummy with Eidervik than she had made out? He was being asked to commit a felony, and if the police got wise to it, he would be prevented from interfering further. Was that the game, or was she really playing a lone hand? If not Eidervik, was there someone else behind her?

Either way he might be walking into a

trap. But the sheer uncertainty was an impetus in itself, an impetus that couldn't be denied. Dangerous opportunities had a habit of presenting themselves to him, and if he had failed to grasp them, regardless of the consequences, he would not have been Peter Gayleigh.

He leaned forward, started the engine again and released the handbrake in a symbolic gesture.

'Okay, let's get moving.' As an after-thought he added: 'If you don't mind I'll listen in while you phone Eidervik. It should be amusing.'

And advisable, he thought!

3

The house in Charles Street, like so many in Mayfair, had been converted into flats. It differed in no way from its Georgian contemporaries on either side, and at any other time he wouldn't have given it a second glance. As it was, he hadn't taken his eyes off it for the past ten minutes. Neither had the girl, and with mounting impatience. They were waiting some fifty yards away, the Jaguar having been parked in a side street.

'He should have left by this time,' she frowned. 'He sounded eager enough on the phone.'

'So it seemed. Maybe he's still sprucing himself up for the occasion. Not to worry. This, I feel, is your lucky night.'

'It should be yours, too. If you hadn't met me — '

'I know,' he said. 'And if you hadn't shown such enterprise I hate to think what would have happened. I'm not belittling all you've done — far from it. You've done so much I feel your efforts should be rewarded. They will be, I'm sure!'

The phone call to Eidervik had been made from Peter's flat. Partly because he had no intention of letting her out of his sight while collecting his tool-belt, which, he had gathered would be required on this jaunt. Already, he was prepared to bet, she had tried everything short of force to open her boy friend's bureau.

Suddenly he felt the pressure of her

fingers on his arm.

'There he is — leaving now!'

A tall, robust figure had emerged from the house, pausing for a few moments to light a cigar before striding briskly away in the opposite direction. Whether that pause, the flare of a match, was deliberate or not they could scarcely have missed it. To Gayleigh it was a tantalising, though not discouraging thought.

'He always smokes cigars,' she said.

'Does he indeed!'

He had turned the corner of the street when they reached the front door. It was closed and locked, but presented no problem to the girl. She had a key, opening it quickly and leading the way to a flat on the ground floor. Here, she produced the key he had seen before, Peter wondering how many more of them she had. Quite a collection, he surmised, if she always showed such interest in her men friends' belongings.

As she slipped into the small, dark hallway of the flat, he followed quickly, closing the door quietly behind them.

'Don't switch on the light,' he told her.

'Better this way.'

The torch he took from his tool-belt showed him two doors leading off to his right. The far one was slightly ajar, and she was pointing to it.

'The bureau is in there.'

It was a sitting-room, he saw, as he went up to it, peering in — a room which reflected the sybaritic tastes of the man, or possibly those of a long line of mistresses to whom he had pandered. A white bear skin rug nestled against the foot of a divan on which there was a liberal supply of cushions. A gilt standing-lamp overlooked this cosiness, the coral pink shade matching the tiled fireplace, and the heavy plush curtains drawn over the window. The Chippendale table and chairs were very elegant, in marked contrast to the very solid looking mahogany bureau facing the still warm electric radiator set at waist level in the fireplace.

'H'm, you go for this sort of decor?' Peter said, pulling a face.

'No, not me. It was all in situ by the time he got round to me. He has a flair for entertaining women, mostly the starry eyed budding starlet type. They think he's aesthetic — until they learn differently. He's far from being a sissy.'

'As you found out.'

'No, I had him figured from the start. But I was at a loose end when I met him, as I told you. I'll try anything for a fresh experience. Do you think you can open the bureau without making too much noise?'

He crossed to the bureau, and began to examine it, tapping it with his knuckle. Under the polished wood there must be a strong metal framework, he realised, the locks of the drawers embedded in it.

'I wonder why he keeps it in here?' he said.

'So that he could always keep his eye on it, I fancy — even when he was busy with other distractions. Well, what do you think?'

'It's a matter of time, that's all.'

He took a tapering steel jemmy from his tool-belt and set to work, testing, prodding, and levering as she held the torch for him. Other tools came into use as the minutes passed, his strong fingers and supple wrists moving with fascinating expertise. He was working with a heavier tool with a slotted handle and taking a cross piece when she asked tensely: 'How much longer?'

'It's tougher than I expected.' He was breathing heavily with exertion. 'Triple locks and heavy complicated mechanism. There's bound to be some noise, I'm afraid.' He indicated the room door. 'You'd better shut that.'

He waited until she had done so, then flexed his muscles and swung down on the lever. There was a harsh rasping sound that made her wince. The lock was yielding, but the drawer didn't budge. He was working on the top drawer, and there were four others, only one of which might disclose the secret project in which this Norwegian was involved. It seemed more than likely that he kept all his personal papers in the bureau, those of a more general nature, and of little interest right now.

This consideration had evidently occurred to the girl.

'Suppose what we're looking for isn't in that drawer?' she said.

157

'Then we'll have to try the others. Just keep your fingers crossed.'

She shot an anxious glance towards the door. 'He could be back before we manage it. My God, I need a drink!' And she switched the torch light away from him towards a cocktail cabinet.

'Not *now!*' he snapped. This was a fine time for such diversions!

'I must. I can't stand much more of this . . . Just a quick one.'

She certainly looked as if she needed something to steady her nerves, he thought, waiting impatiently while she poured herself a stiff whisky, gulping some of it down. Then with the glass in her hand she came back to him, directing the torch on to the bureau again.

'To resume,' he said dryly.

He adjusted the heavy tool he was using, and applied more leverage. There was the protesting note of steel against steel, but this time it terminated in a rending sound. The lock had finally yielded.

'At last!' she exclaimed eagerly, bending closer.

He was pulling the drawer open when

the room was suddenly flooded with light.

Osvald Eidervik stood in the open doorway, one hand on the electric switch, the other wrapped about an automatic.

4

He was blond and beefy, a man in his early forties with heavy features which in a few years would add a multiplicity of chins. Already his neck bulged over his collar, the bullock-like torso tapering down to well-filled trouserlegs and surprisingly small, dapper feet. Despite his bulk he looked as if he could move very quickly.

'So! The impudent Mr. Gayleigh.' The throaty words carried a pronounced foreign accent. 'Drop those tools. You will then raise your hands.'

Peter did that, glancing sharply from Eidervik to the girl, cursing himself for a fool. She had now moved away from him, staring at the Norwegian with expectancy in which there was no trace of concern. Moreover he wasn't covering her with the gun. He didn't seem to think it was necessary.

The thick lips tugged down as he took a couple of steps into the room.

'I gather you didn't expect me,' he said grimly. 'In this country you have a saying: two is company three is none.'

'There's another one,' Peter retorted, looking at the girl again. 'Birds of a feather flock together. Nice work, Corinne!'

'You think I fixed this?' she said, scowling. 'Don't be ridiculous. How could I have done?'

Though he could find no answer to that, the thought still persisted. The way she had looked at Eidervik . . .

The Norwegian had condescended to notice her now.

'You do her an injustice,' he said sourly. 'The only reason she helped you was because she was also helping herself. Unfortunately I have had some experience of Miss Raeburn, and I have found she is made that way. When I received her phone call I was not deceived.'

Peter said: 'Your shrewdness amazes me! But, of course, I should have known.

You're a highly educated intelligent man, a biologist, I believe.'

'We are not here to discuss my profession,' was the reply.

'Nor your latest research on women.'

Eidervik's grip tightened on his gun.

'That, too, is beside the point,' he frowned. 'We are here because I heard you had been busy in Hampstead tonight. My colleague Maynard phoned me. In the circumstances I decided it would not be advisable to leave my flat for long. I shall now do my duty as an honest, law abiding citizen. The police can deal with you both.'

His fleshy eyes darted to the girl, moving on to a telephone standing on an occasional table near the divan.

'Go back and stand over there, by your accomplice.'

That he meant every word of it was only too apparent. Whatever his secret, shared with Maynard and Shirley Quentin, he had no fear of the police. And from the way he was handling the gun he seemed to be much more of a realist than Maynard. Obviously he intended to keep both his intruders at a very safe distance.

'I said stand over there,' he repeated with greater emphasis, as the girl hesitated. 'If either of you are in doubt I shall not hesitate to prove to you that I am an excellent shot.'

'You'd shoot a woman?' she said, her lips curling.

'I have two eyes, my dear. A woman did you say? Right now I can see only a thieving bitch.'

'I always knew you were a swine,' she retorted, her green eyes glinting.

Peter cocked a reproving eyebrow.

'Dear me,' he said. 'I thought you'd had your private quarrels. Do let's keep the party clean! I think you'd better do as he says, Corinne.'

Once she was standing beside him, he thought, he might get the chance to reach the gun in her pocket. It might not get him out of this spot, but it was worth a try. Better in his hand than hers — if she had any intention of using it, which he was still inclined to doubt. On her own admission she had been pretty thick with Eidervik.

He was quite unprepared for what actually happened, though not slow to take advantage of it. Her shoulders lifted in a shrug, her breath coming fast as she stared down at the glass still in her hand. Then without a word she took one step towards him — before she swung round with panther-like swiftness making a desperate dash for the door. Since Eidervik was standing near it he had no difficulty in grabbing her arm, jerking her back.

A rather foolish, futile, effort on her part, Peter thought, until he realised the motive behind it. The whisky in her glass. At such short range she couldn't miss — as she flung the spirit straight into the Norwegian's face.

Half-blinded, he clamped a hand to his smarting eyes, the gun pointing aimlessly. And that was all the incentive Peter needed. He was across the room in less than a second, his fist shooting out and connecting squarely with Eidervik's solar plexus. He gave a pig-like grunt and doubled up. Or rather he would have done if Peter hadn't stopped him. He did this very effectively with two combination punches that rocketed up to lose their impetus on the Norwegian's flabby chin.

He went down like a stunned ox, and would probably have made nearly as much noise if Peter hadn't caught him as he fell. He deposited him on the carpet in an inert and rather untidy heap before returning to the bureau to collect his tools. He didn't need to look in the partly open drawer. He had already seen that it contained nothing but headed notepaper and envelopes.

'My, my, you're quite a man!' Corinne said. 'I wouldn't have missed that for any-thing!'

'Thanks for giving me the opportunity. Now we'll get out of here.'

She knit her brows, blinking at him.

'You don't mean you're giving up? But why? We could use his gun when he comes round.'

It was on the tip of his tongue to say: 'Why bother, we could use yours!' Instead he said: 'We could commit robbery, arson, and murder, and what have you. But we're not going to. Both Maynard *and* Eidervik were much too anxious to phone the cops for my liking. They seem to have a corner in righteousness. As for you, my sweet, I'm damned if I know what side you're on. Anyway, we're leaving right now.'

'So you still don't trust me,' she said, giving him a scathing look. 'My God, what more must I do to convince you I hate this fat beast!'

'Nothing at present. I've had enough for tonight, if you haven't. We'll leave him with his gun and his mortification. Now get moving.'

To assist her he gripped her arm firmly — the arm which might have produced her hidden pistol — took the empty whisky glass from her hand, set it down, and urged her to the door. She made no further protest, eyeing him in sullen silence as he hurried her along the short hallway and out of the flat.

They had reached the street when she said with every evidence of disgust. 'I still think we missed a splendid opportunity. I don't believe in half-measures.'

'Frankly, neither do I. Not as a rule, but circumstances alter cases. I think it would be far safer for everyone concerned if I took you home.'

'No thanks.' Her green eyes flashed fire. 'Nobody orders me about. I'll go alone. As for you, Mr. Gayleigh, you can go to hell.'

And she swung round on her heel her chin held high as she walked away, Peter gazing after her speculatively. Irresponsible she might be, reckless and self-willed she certainly was. But he had seldom met a girl who intrigued him so much. Her spirit appealed to him, if not her intentions.

He went back to his car, slid into the driving seat, and lit a contemplative cigarette. By now Eidervik could be reviling him over the telephone to the police. Even if he wasn't, Maynard could have bleated out a similar complaint earlier.

He had a nasty feeling they had really meant what they said. By accident or design the over zealous Miss Raeburn had got him into quite a spot.

Did Maynard and Shirley Quentin know she had been having an affair with

Eidervik? Possibly not. They might know nothing about her, in which case he had some information to trade. A further request for an interview with Shirley might not be met with a point blank refusal. If he was glib enough he might manage it.

Sheer optimism? Maybe it was. But Fate sometimes smiled favourably on buccaneers with built-in persistance. Anyway, he had nothing to lose by calling on her. It might conceivably be more progressive than avoiding his own flat, which he had every intention of doing. Already the minions of the Law could be waiting for him there!

He began to drive in the direction of Earls Court.

That he had been most unwise he realised almost as soon as he reached her flat. For he had barely thumbed the front door bell when it was answered by the maid, a tall man who bore the unmistakable imprint of officialdom standing immediately behind her.

'Mr. Gayleigh, I believe,' the man said sombrely.

'Yes, I'm afraid so.'

'I understand you've been very busy tonight, sir.' His tone was sardonic as he added: 'Perhaps you could now spare us a little time. I am a police officer, and I must ask you to accompany me. Chief-Superintendent Herrington would like to have a word with you!'

4

1

Herrington's office at Scotland Yard was not unfamiliar to Peter Gayleigh. In the past he had gone there voluntarily and, as on this occasion, by compulsion. Invariably he had been shown into that room for one reason — to impart information concerning his movements. Now he had the certain feeling that it would be unnecessary, that Herrington already had it — and a great deal more information besides, which, as usual, he had kept to himself.

'Sit down, Gayleigh,' he said, with an ominous frown, nodding towards a chair facing his desk.

Peter did that, Herrington staring at him silently.

'Mind if I have a cigarette?' he asked conversationally. 'There are times when I need moral support.'

Since this brought no response he took the liberty of lighting one, blowing out an evanescent stream of smoke which, he felt, was just about as stable as his present position. Then as Herrington continued to stare at him: 'I don't see your whip. Do you keep it in a drawer?'

Herrington said: 'Don't try to be clever. I'm not in the mood, Gayleigh.'

'It used to be Peter. Remember?'

The reminder was ignored.

'A few days ago,' he said steadily, 'I called on you as a friend. I gave you certain information which I hoped you would use. As a result you drove up to Scotland, as I fully expected you would. I credit you with some intelligence.'

'For those kind words many thanks.'

'But since I'd taken you into my confidence I expected a report from you when you got back. Instead — '

'Taken me into your confidence!' Peter's eyebrows had shot up. 'You must be joking. Really, Herrington, do let us try to be honest with each other — for a change! All you did was whet my appetite. A meatless bone tossed to a dog.'

'A dog which bit me,' Herrington retorted sourly. 'As you know, I could fling the book at you. Burglary and assault. What have you got to say?'

'Nothing very much. I — er — gather my victims phoned you.'

'They phoned me.'

'I see . . . ' He eased the ash from his cigarette. 'I admit I was a little head-strong. Sometimes I get carried away with enthusiasm — especially when I'm only given half a story. You'll forgive me if I stress that again.'

Herrington cast a jaundiced glance at the wall clock, one of some 760 slave clocks operated by a battery powered impulse in the new Scotland Yard building. It was getting late, after ten, and he was tired.

'The point *I* am stressing,' he pursued caustically, 'is that I expected some co-operation from you. As it is, I've had to smooth things over with Maynard and Eidervik. It wasn't easy after your misguided efforts.'

'A purely selfless gesture on my behalf, of course!'

Herrington looked at him hard again.

'If you'd consulted me I could have saved you the trouble of calling on them, to say nothing to Miss Quentin. Both these men are highly qualified biologists, biochemists to be more exact. They form part of a team. What they are doing is in the national interest.'

'In other words they aren't villains.' Peter nodded, pursing his lips. 'I rather gathered that.'

'All you've done so far is cause a hell of a lot of trouble. You can thank your lucky stars their complaints came to me.'

'*Why* did they come to you, and not the divisional police?'

'Because their work is top secret. In the event of any interference they had instructions to contact me.'

'I see. But that doesn't quite answer my question, does it? How do you come into this?'

'I, too, have my instructions,' was the non-committal reply.

'Which concern me, of course. When you came to my flat and gave me that spiel about Vincent Stroud and Shirley

172

Quentin, you knew she was engaged to Alan Sinclair, didn't you, and that I knew him fairly well. You also figured that after you left that barograph chart for me to find, I'd shoot up to Scotland, make some excuse to stay with him, and see what I could find out.'

Herrington said without batting an eyelid: 'And what did you find out?'

'Briefly, that Sinclair has hidden depths. Though he spun me a phoney story about being employed by the Forestry Commission I discovered he's in cohoots with a bearded foreigner called Gundersen who operates at Castle Dreich. As your stooge, I did some snooping round those parts, as you intended. No don't worry, I wasn't seen. But now, I think, it's your turn. I'm still waiting to hear what goes on there.'

2

Herrington leaned forward, clasping his hands on his desk. 'All right, I'll tell you — as I could have done much earlier today,' he added, with no more than a trace of his former irritation. 'Professor Theodore Gundersen is a Norwegian, like Osvald Eidervik, who was his assistant when they were working together in a laboratory near Stavanger. As I understand it, they were doing research on micro organisms — something to do with chromosomes — when they suddenly realised they were on the way to creating, if that's the word, a particularly interesting virus.'

'A virulent one, you mean?' Peter interposed quickly. 'One that could be used in germ warfare?'

Herrington nodded grimly.

'Unfortunately they only discovered that later. They didn't realise its potentialities until they published a scientific paper on the subject and had done more research. All this was more than a year ago. Then, much to their consternation, they caught a glimpse of prowlers snooping about near their laboratory. It happened more than once. Incidentally, the deadly possibilities of this virus were first pointed out to them by an English biochemist with whom they'd been exchanging ideas.'

'So it was partly a Norwegian, partly a British discovery.'

'Exactly. Both our Ministry of Defence and the Norwegian equivalent became very interested, of course. They weren't the only ones!' he added significantly.

'I'm following you. Go on.'

'Well the upshot of it was that Gundersen and Eidervik were smuggled out of Norway to this country, together with all their experimental data. And since this had now become an Anglo-Norwegian project somewhere had to be found for Gundersen to continue his research. He was the Norwegians' white-headed boy, and they weren't going to have him working in one of our research centres along with our chaps. They insisted that a new laboratory must be set up where he could carry out his experiments in absolute secrecy.'

Peter nodded. 'Which brings us to Castle Dreich.'

'Yes. Dr. Quentin was approached. He's a biologist himself and knew Professor Gunderson by repute — that he was a brilliant biochemist. He was prevailed upon to co-operate, and as he knew what chemical apparatus would be required supervised its installation after the necessary architectural alterations had been made to the Castle itself. Then when all had been arranged and Gunderson was in residence, the Doctor left for a small village in the South of England where he is now living under another name.'

'I see . . . ' Peter stubbed out his cigarette. 'But there's an odd sort of creature called Gregory living at the castle. How does he fit into this?'

'Gregory?' Herrington's set expression relaxed slightly. 'Oh, there's nothing mysterious about *him*. He was Quinton's man of all work. He's been at Castle Dreich ever since he was a boy. I gather he's a bit simple in some ways. Deformed, too, I believe. The doctor took him under his wing and Gregory worships him and his daughter. Since everyone in those parts knows that he lives there it was thought inadvisable, for the sake of appearances, to remove him.

He doesn't understand what the Professor is doing, but he regards him as his master's friend and makes an excellent watch-dog. From what I've heard he'd be a very useful man to have around in case any strangers became too interested in Castle Dreich.'

In his mind's eye Peter saw the grotesque, bulging face of the dead motor-cyclist in the loch. Apparently Herrington hadn't been told about that. Seemingly, he was only on the perimeter of this very secret business, his duty confined to the London end.

'As I expect you've realised by now,' he resumed, 'Sinclair is our Defence Ministry's man up there. He keeps in very close touch with Gundersen.'

'And Shirley Quentin keeps in touch with them both!'

'Yes.'

'Ostensibly to visit her father at her old home. This thing has been thought out pretty well.'

'We hope so. She was recruited as a very suitable messenger. When she returns to London she carries a coded record of

Gundersen's latest progress to Maynard, for our people, and to Eidervik for the Norwegian Embassy. For strict security reasons neither of them have been told where Gundersen's laboratory is situated. They are forbidden to meet, and both of them only receive part of the information the girl brings. They read it and make suggestion for further experiments which reach Gundersen through the top security men. Vincent Stroud was our Ministry's representative down here, before he vanished and was found murdered, poor devil!'

'In other words,' Peter said dryly, 'something went wrong with these security measures. Might I ask one simple question? Why are you so keen to involve me in all this? I have a shrewd suspicion I'm being used to attract the attention of some very ugly birds — and to hell with what happens to me when they get busy!'

Herrington had the grace, he noticed, to look just a trifle disconcerted, the back of his jacket collar edging up over his neck as he hunched his shoulders.

'The Powers that Be thought you were just the man,' he said somewhat feebly.

'Because I have the reputation of poking my nose in where it's not wanted?'

'Well, to some extent — yes. The opposition will be inclined to think you got into this thing entirely on your own. That you have no official connections.'

Peter said with a grimace: 'How nicely you put it. You mean I'm to be out on a limb. If, while I'm engaged in this performance, I'm bumped off, everyone on your side of the gate says: 'What a pity! We used him as bait and he was gobbled up — but better him than one of our chaps!''

'You've never been afraid to take risks,' was the sardonic reply. 'So come off it. I know, and you know, that I've got you hooked. I recommended you for this job, and quietly you're just loving it.'

As it was only too true, Peter lit another cigarette. You couldn't kid Herrington.

'This opposition you mentioned . . . ' he said, brushing away a cloud of smoke. 'Where does it spring from? Do you know?'

Herrington shook his head, his voice taut again.

'I only wish we did. All we do know is that Gundersen and Eidervik had barely been smuggled over here before another biochemist disappeared from a laboratory in East Germany. This man, the Herr Doktor Ulrich von Shroeder, was a member of Himmler's secret police during the war, and was entirely ruthless. The years haven't mellowed him, and it's possible his disappearance might have something to do with the Gundersen project — and the Russians! He's a good organiser, and very handy with a gun.'

'You think he could be over here?'

'It's possible. Our top people don't know. But they do know that information about this virus has been leaking out. There could be a traitor in the nest — and that doesn't exclude Sinclair or even his fiancée. That's why I didn't put you wise to all this before you went to Scotland. He wasn't told that you'd be coming, of course. Gundersen didn't know, and neither did his fellow boffins.'

He frowned, leaning back slowly in his desk-chair.

'Listen, Peter. The reason you found

one of my men at the Quentin girl's flat was because she hadn't returned there after leaving Maynard's house tonight, though her maid — another of our people — expected her. She hasn't shown up even yet, or I should have been informed.' He paused momentarily, glancing towards the telephones on his desk. 'It's damned queer, all the more so as she's vanished tonight — after you started sticking your oar in so obviously. Of course she may turn up with some quite simple explanation. But I'm worried. I suppose you didn't see any sign of her after she left Maynard's house?'

Peter shook his head. 'No, I didn't. She left by the back way. I made a very undignified exit through the front door, as I expect Maynard told you.'

'Yes . . . He also told me that you'd both heard someone sneaking along the hall. Whoever it was scarpered pretty quickly. Maynard didn't catch a glimpse of this intruder, but maybe you did?'

'No, it was as black as ink outside.' Not a muscle betrayed his thoughts.

'H'm. And you saw nothing after

Maynard slammed the door behind you?'

'Not a thing, Herrington.' He met his gaze very directly and with every semblance of sincerity. 'Nobody was hareing away along the crescent when I got there. I'd say the man nipped round into the back garden and slipped off that way.'

'Yes, I suppose so. If only you'd got your hands on him!'

There was a pause, Peter waiting for him to get round to Corinne Raeburn. Herrington would want to know where he had met her, since he had not gone to Eidervik's flat alone. Actually, he was rather surprised that Herrington hadn't asked him this very pertinent question much earlier.

He didn't ask it now. He made no reference to her as he went on. None at all. Which was unnatural — unless Eidervik hadn't mentioned her when making his complaint. If so, why not? Had his affair with her been kept secret? Now he came to think of it and in view of what he had just been told, it was unlikely that Eidervik would have been permitted to form such a dangerous liaison.

Herrington spoke as if he knew nothing about it, simply referring to his previous remark.

'Taking this snooper into account I fancy you'll be receiving more attention from the opposition very shortly.' He looked at the wall-clock again. 'All right, that's all. But mind you keep in touch with me in future. You'd better!'

Peter said, as he rose: 'Thanks for your advice. Now that I've been thoroughly briefed, I take it I can go. With all this coming and going I haven't had any dinner yet.'

'Neither have I,' Herrington returned gruffly. 'Oh, there's just one more thing,' he said, a glint in his eye. 'That tool-belt you're wearing. Take it off and give it to me. If you were seen leaving here with it I should never live it down!'

Since he had no choice Peter unbuckled it, handing it over with a very tight-lipped expression. He had prized that tool-belt.

'I consider this a very unfriendly act, Herrington.'

'But necessary.' He was smiling wickedly now. 'I'll put it in the drawer where I keep my whip.'

Peter said, looking at him hard: 'Very funny!' To himself he added: 'You'll pay for this, brother.' He bid him a rather terse good night, and went out. Some dignity had to be preserved.

Back in his Jaguar, in which he had been escorted to the Yard, he headed towards Charles Street. On the way he did some more thinking. Corinne Raeburn and Eidervik. He thought he wouldn't be surprised if they were together again.

But if they were, he saw no sign of it when he reached Eidervik's flat. It was in darkness. Nobody there, apparently. As he lit another cigarette it occurred to him that a further inspection might not have been unproductive. Here was the opportunity, but since he had been deprived of his tool-belt he couldn't take advantage of it. Rather a pity. Herrington could be very aggravating at times.

He began to think about Corinne Raeburn again, his ace in the hole. Where did she live? Unfortunately she hadn't told him, but the telephone directory should remedy that deficiency, also, he thought, he might have another job for that ever willing little man Albert.

There was a public call-box not far away. Hopefully he drove towards it.

3

It was early next morning when she came . . .

He had barely finished breakfast when the front door bell rang. Carver answered it, and Peter heard a woman's voice.

Corinne Raeburn!

He tossed the morning paper he had been reading aside, and rose, an expectant gleam in his cool blue eyes. Very kind of her! Could it be that Herrington's prediction was already about to be fulfilled?

She came into the room rather hesitantly, and with a tiny apologetic smile.

'I expect you're surprised to see me?' she said.

Peter admitted that he was. She looked very different this morning. Very attractive. Gone was the anorak and the dark skirt. Now she was wearing a very smart twopiece, suitable for travelling, the colour matching her eyes. A pair of very expensive low-heel sling-backs added to the shapeliness of her legs, if that were possible.

He offered her a chair, and a cup of coffee which she declined saying she had already had breakfast.

'I thought that after our disagreement last night — ' he was beginning more appositely, when she interrupted him.

'Yes, I know. But since then I've been thinking things over.'

'Have you indeed?'

She nodded, undeterred.

'I'm convinced there's something shady going on, and I feel I've simply got to get to the bottom of it.'

'Good for you,' he said. 'There's nothing like determination.' It was not enough to be a *femme fatale*, he thought. Sometimes you had to behave as if you were a dare-devil, but eager to help other people. Specifically, himself.

'You didn't tell me much last night, did you?' she said, seemingly puzzled. 'I've been wondering how you got involved in this thing. Was it purely by chance, as I did?'

'Starting with Osvald, you mean?'

The voluptuous lips tightened.

'There you go again,' she said. 'Questions, nothing but questions! I was absolutely frank with you last night, yet you persist in doubting me. I simply can't understand why. If I hadn't used that whisky to such good effect I don't know what would have happened to us.'

Peter said: 'I think I do. Our Mr. Eidervik looked very much in earnest.'

'Of course he was. He's a sadistic beast, and he'd have used that gun. He had no intention of phoning the police — he daren't. Surely that must be obvious to you now? If he had done, after we left, I wouldn't be here. Neither would you. We should have been arrested by now. So he must be mixed up in something illegal.'

If she was only what she professed to be, the logic behind this would have been unassailable, he thought, admiring the way she had put it. When it came to dissimulation this girl was good. There was no denying it — just as there was no denying she had used him for target practice outside Maynard's house, after sneaking inside. He hadn't forgotten that, or the fact that Eidervik had said nothing about her to Herrington.

But as she wasn't supposed to know he had been picked up — well, two could play at this double game.

He said, as though accepting her argument: 'Yes, I've been thinking about that.'

'Maynard or that Quentin girl couldn't have phoned the police either.'

'No, that's right. It stands out a mile, doesn't it.' He looked at her rather sheepishly. 'As I said, I've been thinking, and I owe you an apology, Corinne. I was wrong about these people. They must be up to something fishy. Are you sure you won't have some coffee?'

She smiled. She said, as one who had made her point, and could forgive: 'Well, perhaps a small cup, and now that's cleared up I'd like a cigarette.'

Cheered with this new found matey-ness, established on both sides, he went to the door, calling out to Carver to bring another cup and saucer. Then in the meantime supplied her with the cigarette.

As he lit it he said, his eyes smiling as they held hers: 'Even I can make a mistake. All right, no heel taps, darling. Like you I got into this business entirely on my own. When the Ungodly are around I usually do.'

'That's more like the Peter Gayleigh I've heard about,' she emphasised, lowering her silky eyelashes as she added slyly: 'The man who knows all about women — or thought he did. I was damned annoyed with you last night.'

Peter didn't say he had noticed it. He apologised again, and Carver having supplied the necessary, helped her to the cup of coffee. He was handing it to her when she put her earlier question more directly. How had it come about that he had gone to Maynard's house, she wanted to know.

'Simple because Shirley Quentin is

engaged to a friend of mine,' he told her. 'She seemed to be gallivanting around more than somewhat — and not with her fiancé. On different occasions I spotted her at the *Green Mask* with both Maynard and Eidervik. Just as you did, except that I happened to be eating there. I wondered what she was up to, and — '

'And being Peter Gayleigh you thought you'd try to find out,' she completed. 'When you were pumping me last night you mentioned the name Sinclair. That must have been Alan Sinclair.'

'Yes. But I got the impression you didn't know him.'

'I don't,' she said. 'But I read the papers, and I've a pretty good memory.'

'The engagement announcement?'

She nodded, her lips pursed.

'This girl's father lives at a castle in Perthshire. I couldn't remember its name at first, a very unusual name. Then it came back to me. It's called Castle Dreich.'

4

Suddenly there seemed to be a stillness in the room, though she had simply paused to drink some of her coffee. There was nothing more than keen interest in her face, but he felt his pulse tingling. He thought the guileless way in which she had mentioned the name was quite artistic.

'Is that important?' he said.

'Yes, I'm almost sure it is.'

He shrugged. He said: 'Sorry, I don't see the connection.'

She settled herself more comfortably in the chair, crossing her elegant legs and leaning back, her cigarette poised between her fingers. At that moment, he thought, she looked like the cat that had stolen the cream.

'I think I'm on to something.' It was uttered with an air of achievement. 'We've scared them all right. Wait till I tell you.'

'Tell me what? I must say you look very pleased with yourself.'

'I am.' She leaned forward again, taking a quick draw at her cigarette. 'Listen,

Peter, Eidervik's taken to his heels. I know he has, and I've a good idea where he's gone.'

'Eidervik?' He looked at her sharply. 'No?'

She nodded emphatically.

'After I left you last night I didn't go far away. I felt I had to convince you somehow that I was on the level. Also I wanted to see if a police car pulled up outside his flat — I was almost sure he wouldn't carry out his threat, you see. He didn't of course. And while I was waiting near the end of Charles Street I saw him leave — with a suitcase.'

'You did?'

'Huh-huh. He took a taxi and I grabbed another one and followed him. He went to Euston and I saw him get on the night train to Glasgow. Actually, he booked through to Stirling as I found out from the ticket-collector. And,' she added triumphantly, 'that's almost on the border of Perthshire. Now do you see the connection?'

Peter did, only too well, and with an increased feeling of awareness. Was this part of her story true? Eidervik's flat had certainly been in darkness when he had returned there. If it wasn't true what was the point of it?

'H'm.' He rubbed his chin. 'But it doesn't necessarily follow he's gone to Castle Dreich?'

'It's a damn good bet he has, since he was so thick with this Quentin girl. Anyway I'm going to find out. I'm taking the Glasgow express — this morning. It leaves around ten o'clock. *I'm* going to Castle Dreich, and nobody is going to stop me,' she told him very earnestly.

'I still think it's a long shot.'

'Well, I don't. That's why I've called so early. If you're as interested as I think you are, you'll want to come with me.'

So here it was! By agreeing to her suggestion he could be walking into danger. A trap that had been subtly prepared. He was almost sure of it. But not quite sure. The whole of her story, right from the moment he had met her, *could* be true. It didn't follow that because she had amused herself sadistically at his expense outside Maynard's house that she was still pally with Eidervik. No it didn't. And she had always been one for seeking excitement, according to her reputation.

Yes, the slight, the very slight element of uncertainty was there, whispering temptingly to him. Yet even if it hadn't been so he would have found the challenge behind her words irresistible. He was made that way, and she knew it, of course.

'Well?' A glance at her wrist-watch, and she rose purposefully, putting her coffee cup down. 'It's after nine now. Do we go together, or must I go alone?'

'If there's one thing that gets me it's gentle persuasion,' he said dryly. 'I'm a sucker for it. I bet you've already packed your suitcase?'

'Yes.' She nodded briefly and emphatically. 'I've simply to pick it up. Are you coming with me?'

'Need you ask. Gallantry forbids me to let a lady go alone.'

'I knew you wouldn't disappoint me,' she said, with obvious satisfaction. 'As I said last night, we're two of a kind, Peter.'

And she came up to him placing her hands on his broad shoulders, her perfume strong in his nostrils again. 'We could be very close, you and I.'

'At this very moment,' he said, a twinkle in his eye, 'I am fighting a natural inclination. I expect you can guess what it is. But I never allow myself to be seduced immediately after breakfast.' He removed her hands gently. 'Besides, you have a bag to collect, and I may need a few clothes myself. Also, I'll have to cancel a luncheon date, among other things. Now be off with you before I weaken. We don't want to miss that train.'

'No . . . ' she said, with a little *moue*. 'But I still think you're playing hard to get. All right, I'll meet you at Euston, outside the platform. Okay?'

He told her it was, and accompanied her to the door of his flat. She had kept a taxi waiting, and he watched her step back into it and drive away. Another taxi parked farther along Jermyn Street was about to follow when he raised a beckoning hand.

The taxi drew up and Albert Orne

looked out through the open window, his wide mouth splitting into a grin.

'Watcher, guv!'

Peter motioned him into the street and drew him aside. Much to the little man's gratification a fiver changed hands.

'Make it fast, Albert. I can only spare a minute.' Last night the windows of her Mayfair flat had been in darkness, like Eidervik's, when he had located her address and gone there. Albert had then taken over.

Now he learned that she had got back soon after he had left. She had not gone out again later that night and had not shown herself that morning, before making her visit to him.

'Sorry I ain't got more to report, guv. What now?'

'Nothing more,' said Peter. 'We can't win all the time. I'll be seeing you, Albert.'

He went quickly back into his flat.

5

A couple of minutes later he was on the phone to Herrington. Not to enlighten him. Oh no! Herrington had dangled him on a string far too long. It was time to cut loose. Even so, the fountainhead of official information must be tapped.

'I thought I'd give you a tinkle,' he said dutifully. 'Any further news about our Miss Quentin?'

'She's still missing,' Herrington told him. 'It's damned queer and very worrying. I thought it possible she'd slipped up to Scotland, but apparently she hasn't.'

Peter said, his tongue in his cheek: 'Maybe she called on Eidervik later last night?'

A grunt came over the line. 'D'you think I haven't tried to contact him? He isn't in his flat. I'm still waiting for him to get back.'

If there was any truth in Corinne's story, Peter thought, he might have to wait a long time.

He said: 'Is that so? I expect he'll be

back. But I must say your chess pieces seem to be getting a little out of hand, Herrington. You'll let me know what transpires? As you said, we must keep in touch.'

Before any reply could reach him he pressed down the receiver-rest, and dialled Diana's number. Though he welcomed danger, impulsiveness must be tempered with a modicum of discretion — especially when you were dealing with a girl like Corinne. Diana, thank God, was very different! *Really* reliable.

'Hullo, honey,' he said. 'Since I saw you yesterday there have been some developments. Quite a few, in fact. I haven't time to explain now. I'm going to be pretty busy. I'm making another trip to Scotland, by train.'

'You mean — you're going to see Sinclair again?'

'Er — no, darling. Herrington has deigned to supply me with some very interesting gen. He knows about the work Sinclair and Gundersen are doing. It's all very hush-hush, but Sinclair can be trusted absolutely. You'll be able to rely on him, Di.'

'Me?' she said, puzzled. 'Rely on him? Why should I?'

'There's something I want you to do — for my sake, my sweet.'

A pause. Then she said:

'Here we go again! What is it now?'

'That's my girl. I want you to warn Sinclair. Unexpected company may be arriving at Castle Dreich. Dangerous company. I think a takeover is more than likely, though I can't be absolutely certain. Just tell him that. No, not over the phone — I need a little time, and there are other considerations, so you'll have to see him personally.'

'But he's in Scotland, isn't he? If you're going there why can't you — ?'

'You never know, I may not get there!'

'You mean you might be prevented?' There was an anxious note underlying her curiosity now. 'Look, Peter — '

'So I want you to take my car and drive up to Bridge of Allan as soon as possible. Got that?' While she was still groping for a reply, he went on: 'Believe me, it's vitally important, otherwise I wouldn't ask you. Whether I reach the castle or not Sinclair will know what to do. No time for more now. You're beautiful, I love you, honey, and you've never failed me. Not a word to Herrington mind, before you set off! Bye now, my sweet.'

And he put the phone down quickly.

Half a minute later it rang. But he didn't answer it, and as it went on ringing told Carver to ignore it. He had more than a hunch that Diana was trying to get through to him again. In fact he was quite sure of it. Pity he couldn't tell her more, but time was pressing.

'Call a taxi for me, Carver,' he said, as he flung some things into a bag. 'I've got to catch a train. How long I shall be away I don't know, but if Mr. Herrington should call today just tell him I've gone out. Er — Miss Caryll will be coming here shortly. She'll be taking my car, so I'll leave you the keys.'

Ten minutes later the taxi was bearing him away. He didn't doubt that Corinne would be waiting for him at Euston, and was not disappointed. He didn't ask her if she had brought her pistol along for the sport ahead.

His own automatic was in the pocket of the raincoat he carried over his arm. At times the weather in Scotland could be most inclement!

Part Three

1

1

'But surely,' she had said, 'there must be some sort of road to this outlandish place?'

'Not that I've seen. The best we can hope for, I'm afraid, is some semblance of a cart track. The Scottish moors, you know, are a bit short on modern conveniences.'

This was after he had told her, with suitable vagueness, that he had seen Castle Dreich away in the distance while touring those parts in his car some time ago. Apparently, she had had no idea where it was situated, only that it was in Perthshire.

'So it's in a very desolate part,' she had said, nodding. 'All the more reason why something shady could be going on there.'

It was becoming a refrain. She was

plugging it hard enough, he thought.

'If Eidervik has gone there, I want to know why,' she went on, frowning. 'And as he never goes anywhere on foot if he can help it, I just can't believe he had to walk across the moor. There *must* be some other way to reach it.'

The journey to Glasgow, relieved by lunch on the train, had been uneventful. With Corinne it could never have been tedious. All her life she had done and got what she wanted, throwing convention to the winds. A spoilt, uninhibited girl who had never lacked money and indulged every wilful persuit that had occurred to her.

At bottom she was immature. People were toys to be discarded, like the men she had known, when she thought fit. Anything for a kick. Nothing was more certain than that her interest in him would fade when he had served her purpose, whatever it was. If she had deliberately lured him to Scotland he failed to understand why. She needn't have called on him. She could have gone on her own. Instead —

It was both puzzling and intriguing, because he didn't think for one moment that it was his reputation and sex appeal that accounted for her interest in him. Her efforts to seduce him had been far too blatant, lacking the subtlety of experience.

In Glasgow they hired a car, a rather ancient Morris 1000, small but suitable for the rough moorland trip ahead of them. They took the A80 to Stirling. Then on, past Bridge of Allan and the crows nesting in the fir trees, past the spot where the motor-cyclist had hidden with his rifle. As yet Diana wouldn't have got to Sinclair's house, since it was barely half-past six.

Doune . . . Callander. Then, under a leaden sky, the frowning hills beyond draped in faint mist. Through the Pass of Leny, bringing them to Loch Lubnaig where the water had lost its blueness, whipped by the breeze into tiny crests breaking mutinously against the banks. Strathyre . . . Balquhidder.

'When do we turn off the main road?' she wanted to know, staring intently ahead.

'In a minute or two,' Peter said. 'We'll take the road along the south bank of Loch Earn.'

'How far then?'

'I'm hoping we shall be able to veer south from there in the general direction of Ben Vorlich.

'Shall we be able to see the castle before we branch off from the Loch?' she asked, with every indication of innocence.

'No, nothing but moorland and glens. It lies in one of them.'

Driving alongside the Loch they came presently to a wide gate which offered a faint track beyond, through the scrub and heather. He pulled up, opened the gate, having assessed their position from the distant Ben Vorlich. 'I think we'll try this, if you're game. Farther on you'll probably find it more bumpy than your first riding lesson.'

'I'm game for anything,' she said.

She looked as if she was, the side windows of the car open, her chestnut hair blown by the wind as she stared out.

Maybe you are, he thought, his hand never far from the pocket of the raincoat he was now wearing, it depends what game you're playing. The dangerous part of this journey was about to begin. Out on those moors, virtually alone, he might simply be asking for trouble.

He got back into the Morris, edged it through the gate, and drove slowly on.

'Traffic in this direction about one cart and sundry sheep per week, I should think,' he remarked.

She said: 'I always think sheep look so stupid, don't you?

'Maybe they'll think we are if this track peters out.'

It was not long before it almost did, the springs of the little car protesting as they rode over the uneven, coarse, grassland. A Land-Rover would have served their purpose better, he thought, if only one had been available, which it hadn't been.

'This buggy ride is a bit like being on Safari. I tried that once,' she said, with undiminished enthusiasm as they bumped and swayed about in their seats. 'It was great fun.'

'I'm glad you think this is.'

'This is different. We're man-hunting

this time. Which reminds me, I have a pistol I brought along. Since Eidervik had a gun I thought it might be useful. I packed it away in my bag if you'd like to see it?'

Such disarming frankness. Peter looked at her, meeting the guileless keenness in her eyes.

'Not just now,' he said. 'Later. I can't really believe there's all that much danger, otherwise I'd have brought one myself.'

'You should have done,' she replied, shaking her head regretfully. 'I tell you we're after big game.'

Peter shrugged, as if dubiously. The car bumped on.

'How much farther?' she asked presently. 'Surely it can't be far now?'

'In these parts it could be, but I'm hoping it isn't,' he told her, turning the car into a winding glen on their left. This part of the moorland landscape was familiar. He had seen it through his binoculars during the previous trip with Diana. 'By my reckoning the castle can't be more than a mile away now.'

As they were approaching it from a

different direction he wasn't quite sure when they would see it, recalling that it was set low in the hills and partly surrounded by trees. In the far distance a few motionless sheep looked like grey maggots, the quietness of evening claiming the moor. Nothing stirred except an occasional bird on the wing. The sound of the car would carry a long way, he thought. It would be wise to leave it pretty soon.

They had rounded another bend in the narrow glen when it began to broaden out, the terrain becoming much more familiar. He knew exactly where he was now, recognising a ridge on a brae about a third of a mile ahead. It was obliquely opposite the outcrop of rock where he had crouched with Diana.

There were several large boulders topping the crest of the brae, which couldn't be more than a few hundred yards from the castle. A very suitable spot for reconnaisance, after they reached it on foot. He wondered if Gregory would be stationed at the tower window. If so, it would be more reassuring than otherwise.

It could imply that all was well at the castle.

'Okay,' he said, as the car bumped to a halt. 'This is where we start walking. We'll take a look-see from the top of that brae over yonder. Now you'd better get that little gun of yours.'

'You bet!' She was all eagerness now.

He reached behind him, taking her small suitcase from the back seat while she produced the key. She unlocked it and was raising the lid when he glimpsed the pistol lying on top of some filmy underclothes. Before she had time to touch it he had reached out a hand and taken it.

'It's only a small one,' she said, showing no surprise and as if she had expected him to examine it.

'So I see.' It was a German .25, pre-war. A Sauer and Sohn, much less effective than the Walther PPK 8-shot he was carrying. But he considered it much more advisable to have it in his possession than hers.

He turned it over in his hands as if merely inspecting it then put it in the other pocket of his raincoat.

'Hey! What's the idea?' she exclaimed.

'Safer with me,' he said, cocking a disapproving eyebrow. 'I never could trust a girl with a gun — particularly when she's inclined to be hotheaded.'

'But that's ridiculous! I'm a damned good shot.'

'All the more reason why I should keep it. If we meet trouble we don't want you arrested for homicide because you got trigger happy, instead of using that pretty head of yours.'

He smiled as he said it, and though she looked at him sulkily accepted his decision with a shrug. He had expected more protests, more than a suggestion of a fierce glint in those narrowed green eyes. None at all. Merely sulky disappointment. And, of course, she had told him quite openly that she had the gun. So he *could* have misjudged her, the subtlety with which he had credited her all in his own mind. He just didn't know what to think about this high spirited, wayward girl.

Her bag was closed and lying in the

back of the car again together with his own when they set off on foot, the intense silence almost tangible. The few words they exchanged were muttered in undertones. It took them fully ten minutes before they reached a point near and below the ridge he had pointed out. Then a short, steeper climb over the wiry grass towards it.

They were almost there when she quickened her pace eagerly, scrambling up to one of the large boulders ahead of him. Apparently she couldn't see the castle from there, for she looked back at him and shrugged, then rounded the boulder and disappeared from sight.

Such impetuousness, he thought! When he reached it himself, his hand on the Walther in his pocket he saw she had hurried forward to a vantage point offering a view between two taller rocks a few yards farther along the ridge.

She was already peering through, her back towards him, beckoning urgently to him.

It had been extremely well planned, for he was still moving forward, his eyes fixed upon her, when the attack came. His right arm was pinioned, and a split second later his left, by two men who darted from behind the near boulder.

It had also accommodated Osvald Eidervik who was standing only a few feet away from them.

2

Eidervik was wearing a city suit: the two other men leather driving jackets. They were heavily built and muscular, carrying out their work with lightning speed. Caught off his guard, Gayleigh had no hope of defending himself. A chopping blow took him on the back of his neck as his legs were swept from beneath him. In a matter of seconds he was lying face down on the stony ground, both his arms twisted behind him, the Walther he had been clutching wrenched from his grasp. While both men knealt on him, one end of a length of rope was fastened tightly round his wrists.

'Keep him there,' Eidervik said with

infinite disparagement, the corners of his fleshy mouth tugging down. The butt of a gun protruded from his jacket pocket, and he let it remain there since there had been no necessity to use it. 'I have a score to settle with this interloper.'

He moved forward, lashing out viciously with his foot, drawing blood from Gayleigh's unprotected cheek.

'How do you like that, my friend?'

It brought no reply, Peter's head swimming. When he could focus his gaze again he peered up at the girl. She was standing with her hands on her hips, staring down at him with the predatory expression of a stalking cat.

'Thanks very much,' he ground out. 'You're one hell of a bitch, aren't you?'

'Kick him again, for me, Osvald.' She said, her green eyes gleaming with anticipation.

Eidervik did that, Peter stifling a groan. When the mist cleared again he realised the girl had bent over him taking her small automatic from his left hand pocket.

'If you'd looked you'd have seen it

wasn't loaded,' she said. 'You poor fool! This isn't the gun I used last night. A Sauer and Sohn won't take a silencer. But this one does.'

And she jerked up one side of her skirt, showing him a .22 automatic in a holster strapped to the inside of her thigh.

'In case of emergency,' she said scornfully. 'The smart Mr. Gayleigh! I've got a lot of amusement out of you.'

Eidervik said: 'We're wasting time. Get him to his feet.'

Peter was dragged upright, both men stepping away from him as he staggered, one of them pointing the Walther at him the other still holding the other end of the long length of rope. He fastened this round his own waist. The girl and the Norwegian had both stepped well out of their captive's reach.

'We shall now walk,' Eidervik said. 'Since you have shown such interest in Castle Dreich we shall give you the privilege of seeing inside.

'A pleasure I'm sure.' Peter felt a pull on the rope fastening his wrists. 'Just one thing before we set off. How did you know I'd come this way?'

'The outcome would have been the same if you had taken any other route,' was the satisfied reply. 'We should have been waiting for you.'

'Your crystal ball, I suppose?'

'Nothing so archaic.' He turned to the girl. 'Show him, my dear.'

She produced a cigarette-lighter, her lips curling as she held it up. 'Bugged,' she said succinctly. 'VHF. It was sending out signals from the moment we left Loch Earn. Satisfied?'

Peter shrugged. He felt there was little else he could do. With four of them guarding him, ready to counter any ill-considered move he might make his prospects were not bright.

'There's something else I'd like to know — '

'Enough,' Eidervik interrupted, with renewed impatience. 'You will walk ahead of us. If you refuse, you will not be given the opportunity to crawl when Stefan and Ivan have finished you — you will be dragged. We shall proceed?'

'By all means,' said Peter. 'You've made

your point. There are times when I never argue.'

The other two men had the high cheek bones of Slavs, compatriots probably of the motor-cyclist who had ended up in the loch. He wondered where these two had been at the time and whether they always took their orders from the Norwegian. Somehow he doubted it. Despite his air of command, Eidervik looked very much out of his element, the moorland breeze ruffling his very fair hair. His flabby face lacked the strength of a leader, the kind of man who would connive, but scuttle to a bolt hole when the going got tough.

Why had he scuttled from London the previous night? Had his womanising, in the shape of Corinne Raeburn, got him into a situation he wouldn't be able to explain to Herrington. Or didn't that matter. It could be that zero hour had struck, and that everything was going according to plan.

The swarthy character holding the rope gave it another prompting tug, his equally cautious ally jerking the muzzle of the gun away from the two tall rocks immediately ahead. They knew their business, Peter thought. He was to be given no opportunity to dart for shelter, though handicapped as he was, and with three guns against him he had not contemplated such madness.

He walked obediently round the rocks and down the other side of the hill, his narrowed eyes directed towards Castle Dreich not more than three hundred yards away. It looked as inhospitable as before. As far as he could see there was nobody in the watch tower now.

That very fact might have already alerted Alan Sinclair. Maybe it was too much to hope for. But there was always Diana . . .

By the time they reached the more level ground of the deserted glen Eidervik and the girl had ranged themselves on one side of him, the leather-jacketed gunman on the other, the length of rope held taut by the man who came on behind.

'Permission to speak, Miss Raeburn?' Peter asked sardonically.

'You'll get plenty of chance for that

later,' she retorted.

'Indeed! I shall look forward to some enlightening conversation. Would it be too much to ask why you went to the trouble of luring me here? In view of this reception-committee I can't believe it was simply for your perverted amusement. Right now I might still have been in London, wondering where the hell you'd gone.'

'I don't think so,' she said, with a withering glance. 'And neither do you.'

'Why not? You needn't have called on me this morning. You could have made yourself scarce and gone out of my life. Frankly, as things have turned out, I wish you had!'

'I could have done without you, too,' she snapped. 'You and your scruffy accomplice.'

'My accomplice?'

'The little man I saw loitering outside my flat,' she retorted bitingly. 'When I left I knew I should be followed, as I was — to Jermyn Street.'

'I see. And by then you'd decided not to slip off up here alone.'

'What do *you* think? I thought it would

be safer if I had you for company. It wasn't difficult to persuade you. And both of us knew why! Sometimes you're bright, but you're not very clever. Just impulsive — like me,' she reminded him scornfully.

Eidervik, who had been gazing intently towards the castle suddenly captured her attention. He touched her arm, silencing her with a reproving frown, half-pointing to the tower window.

The head and shoulders of a man had appeared there now, a man Gayleigh had never seen before. The wide forehead was topped by closely cropped grey hair, the square cut features spreading out to a heavy jowl. He was standing motionless, staring straight at them, the heavy mask-like face showing none of the weakness of Eidervik's.

Even at a distance this man seemed to exert an hypnotic influence on his captors, Peter noticed. Neither Eidervik nor the girl made any comment. There were no more gibes. Not another word was uttered by any of the other four as they walked on purposefully.

Presently the man moved away from

the window, reappearing a few moments later on the iron stairway leading to the flat roof. A tall, broad-shouldered figure wearing a dark grey, civilian suit. Though the tightly-fitting jacket outlined his girth it didn't detract from his virile appearance. He climbed down, strode past the spot where the helicopter had once stood, and vanished behind the trees farther along.

By this time Gayleigh and his escort were approaching a path, leading beyond the ancient outer wall, to the castle. As they went along it and past the trees he saw that the modern lower building resembled an elongated concrete garage. There were no windows, only a door. A motor-bike and sidecar, and two other motor-bikes were standing outside.

'Professor Gundersen's laboratory, I presume?' Peter remarked.

Eidervik frowned, indicating the door. 'Keep walking.'

They had almost reached it when it opened. The man who had disappeared from the roof stood there, his heavy-lidded eyes hooded as he stared at

Gayleigh. He continued to stare at him in absolute silence, his massive figure almost filling the doorway. Only the girl spoke, and with a respect that was unusual in her.

'He gave us no trouble, Herr Doktor.'

'The English adventurer, hein?' He had scarcely looked at her, uttering the words sourly, and with a thick guttural accent. 'Already he has caused us enough!'

'I don't think I know you,' said Peter. 'An introduction might be in order.'

'Then you shall have one,' was the curt reply. 'My name is Ulrich von Shroeder.'

3

As the name had already been passing through Peter's mind it came as no great surprise — the East German bio-chemist, Herrington had mentioned. He was more surprised that the reply had come without any hesitation. No attempt to conceal his name. This man was very sure of himself.

He turned to the Norwegian. 'The watch-tower,' he said peremptorily. And to the girl: 'You, fraulein, will go back for the car in which you came. Both of you have a lot to learn. Why was it not brought here at once?'

They looked at each other sheepishly. Neither of them said anything, the girl colouring up with unusual embarrassment.

'Bring it now. You have the ignition key?'

'No, Herr Doktor,' she said, very uncomfortably.

'Then get it. You imply this man has not been searched.' He raised his eyes to heaven, as if beset by bungling amateurs. 'You leave a car abandoned in the glen for anyone to see, and — ' For a moment he seemed incapable of words. 'I will deal with Mr. Gayleigh while you attend to the car. Eidervik will signal you from the tower if your mistakes have attracted any attention.'

Nodding silently, she took the ignition key from Gayleigh's raincoat pocket, and hurried back the way they had come. Von Shroeder stood aside, allowing the very subdued Norwegian to pass him. Presumably, he was going to some stairs leading to the roof and the tower.

He had gone when their taskmaster said something in Russian to the other two men. Immediately they came closer, the muzzle of the gun was thrust into the small of Gayleigh's back as the rope was wound tightly round his chest, imprisoning his arms.

'At close quarters I believe you can be dangerous,' Von Shroeder said. 'You will now follow me. If you are troublesome you will be shot.'

He was taken along a short empty passage to a door. Von Shroeder opened it, motioning him through into a laboratory equipped for microbiological research. On one side of it were white plastic containers and several glass retorts. These faced a bench holding a variety of chemical apparatus. The source of electric power was not apparent, though a generator had probably been installed, Peter thought, when the architectural alterations to the castle had been made. At present there was ample light provided by windows in the roof of the laboratory.

Near the door was a black sentinel-like

object that could have been used for X-ray purposes, and not far away from it a model of some complicated molecular structure, the small coloured balls representing atoms, supported on a wire framework.

Peter's gaze had settled on this when the pressure of the gun in his back urged him forward again. At a gesture from von Shroeder he was taken round the far side of the chemical bench to a small office that had not been visible from the door. It had a broad window and as they came up to it he recognised the motionless figure of Professor Gundersen sitting in there.

He was bound to a chair and apparently unconscious, his face bathed in sweat, his mouth contorted, saliva dribbling down his beard. Attached to his wrists and forehead were metal clamps wired to a small box-like object with a dial on a desk nearby.

Electric shock treatment!

Gayleigh's eyes were like frosted glass as he was told to halt. Von Shoeder went into the office. He raised one of the unconscious man's eyelids with his thumb, then struck him smartly across the face. There was no response.

'*Schafskopf!*' he muttered, no pity in his voice, only irritation. 'But you will talk. It is inevitable.' And he snapped his fingers. 'Ivan!'

The man joined him immediately, von Shroeder speaking to him in Russian. A few curt words and the German was again at Peter's side, his underling remaining in the office.

'I dislike such painful methods, Herr Gayleigh. But you have a saying: 'Needs must when the devil drives'.'

'I'm looking at him now.'

The heavy face tightened. 'Possibly you do not appreciate the importance of the Herr Professor's research.'

'To East Germany, or the Soviet Union?'

'They are inseparable,' was the reply. 'What talent I possess is available to both. I admire militant strength. I obey my masters, just as you will obey me.' He cast another glance at Gundersen, and shrugged. 'A brave man but an obdurate fool. When he recovers he will be questioned further. Until then — '

Gayleigh was urged forward again to another door, finding it opened into a room that Gundersen had evidently used as his living quarters, and partly as a study. All the drawers of the bureau were lying open, and a variety of books, technical and otherwise, had been piled on the floor near two empty bookcases. Quite evidently the room had been searched, unavailingly, it would seem, for any written evidence of Gundersen's latest experimental work. 'So you've achieved the final mutation,' Sinclair had said over the scrambler phone only a few days ago. It must, Peter realised, be this information von Shroeder was seeking.

After long months of research on this deadly virus Gundersen's work had been nearing completion.

And now — !

Von Shroeder spoke again in Russian. The man called Stefan handed him the gun, and began to unwind the rope about Gayleigh's chest and arms. Having done so, he carried out a very thorough search for anything that might have served as a weapon. Not content with this he removed all Peter's personal possessions from his pockets, expert fingers exploring his clothes for anything that might have been concealed in the linings of his raincoat and jacket.

'If you look hard enough,' Peter said dryly, 'you'll find a sub-machinegun hidden in the turn-ups of my trousers. I always carry it there.'

Von Shroeder was not amused.

'Ach so! They will be examined for something rather smaller. A safety-razor blade, perhaps? I believe you have been known to secrete such useful objects on your person.'

If it had been there, or anywhere else, it would have been found. Plainly von Shroeder did not believe in half-measures. Peter waited resignedly while his tie was removed and his shirt unbuttoned, the search still proceeding.

'Though I'm hardly in the mood,' he said. 'I'll oblige you by doing a strip tease, if you like.'

'Then you will not need your shoes,' was the sardonic response. 'You will now permit Stefan to take them off.' The levelled gun indicated a chair a few feet away to Peter's right. 'Sit down there.'

Peter shrugged. He turned as if to obey, his hands still tied behind his back. He took one step to his right, a movement which brought the other man between himself and von Shroeder. It was the slim chance he had been looking for.

His muscular shoulder smashed against the Russian sending him reeling back to collide with his leader, Peter's own impetus carrying him to the partly open door only a few yards away. He was kicking it wider open when von Shroeder recovered his balance with disconcerting rapidity. The Walther in his hand barked loudly, a bullet biting into the door within an inch of Gayleigh's head.

'*Halt*! Not that way, my friend!' He spoke with icy deliberation, the gun infinitely menacing. Nothing, it seemed, could ruffle this man for long. He was in complete command of the situation.

4

Peter walked slowly back to the chair and sat down, von Shroeder's hireling glowering at him. The man came across and struck him across the mouth, muttering viciously in Russian.

'Enough!' von Shroeder again. 'We shall now continue.'

Under his direction Gayleigh's ankles were bound together, and his shoes and socks removed, these being carefully examined before von Shroeder was satisfied.

'Now,' he said, 'we can talk. I cannot believe that you were deceived by Fraulein Raeburn's rather obvious trickery. Yet you allowed yourself to be enticed here. Such rashness passes my comprehension. As a biologist, I find you an interesting study.'

Peter said grimly: 'Unfortunately I haven't my microscope, but the feeling is mutual.' An ex-Himmler man, turned chemist, he recalled. An educated man, but with the ingrained traits of his late chief. 'Surely you realise I didn't leave

London without taking certain precautions?'

'You are telling me you advised your friend at Scotland Yard?'

'Naturally.'

'And told him where you were going?' He shook his head. 'Oh no, Herr Gayleigh! I am quite certain you did nothing of the sort. It is not in your adventurous, fool-hardy nature. Moreover it is very clear that you made no mention of Fraulein Raeburn to Chief Superintendent Herrington last night. If you had done, she would not be here now. Your journey today was to be a step into the unknown, and you couldn't resist it. You are a lone wolf with few loyalties.'

Since it was hard to deny, Peter said nothing.

'Fraulein Raeburn has your same wild spirit — as yet untamed! But with training she may make a very good agent. She is financially independent and has social connections. She was recruited quite recently by Eidervik, who, I am afraid will never distinguish himself, though he has been very useful to me.

Money means too much to him. He was too easily bought.'

Peter said: 'It was Eidervik, of course, who kept your people informed of the progress Gundersen was making. Too bad he was only trusted with part of that information. That must have been a great disappointment to you.'

Von Shroeder shrugged, the gun he held, unwavering.

'Difficulties can be overcome. Security measures can be broken. Our main problem was to discover where this laboratory was situated. Unfortunately we were under the impression the girl your Defence Ministry used as a go between was regularly employed as an agent.'

'A professional courier.'

'Ach no. Not nearly so important — simply as a local messenger. To the best of our knowledge the girl never left London. Why should we associate her with a remote castle in Scotland? We were unaware she was Dr. Stewart Quentin's daughter.

'We could have waylaid this girl, but that would have shown our hand and achieved little, since Eidervik already received part of the coded information she carried.'

'In other words you slipped up badly where Miss Quentin was concerned. My heart bleeds for you!'

Von Shroeder's mouth tightened.

'I am not infallible. All of us make mistakes — including you. Gibes are a condemned man's last resort. I can afford to dismiss them for what they are worth. You know too much, Herr Gayleigh. And since we have time on our hands, owing to the Herr Professor's obstinacy, it amuses me to enlighten you further. I gave you my name so readily because you will never repeat it outside this castle.'

Again Peter said nothing. By now Diana must be across the border, well on her way to Bridge of Allan, and Sinclair. She could handle the Jaguar almost as well as he could himself. How much longer?

'This girl, of course,' he went on, as if there had been no interruption, 'was always guarded when she delivered her messages. But we discovered she was in under-cover contact with a professional British agent, a much more important operator. He had many names — '

'One of them Vincent Stroud,' Peter put in promptingly. 'Since we're letting our hair down, maybe you'll tell me why he was liquidated. It's been worrying the hell out of me. I like to get my details right.'

'That much we have in common,' was the stony-faced reply. 'Many months ago now, this girl messenger was temporarily indisposed. She was confined to her flat. And during this short illness the man Stroud made an ill-advised journey. He was, as you say, a very slippery character, and we lost track of him, for a time. We picked him up on the A1 on his return journey. But again he eluded us, having unfortunately recognised me. He had to be eliminated before he could pass on that information. It was attended to at once.'

'So then you were almost back at square one. How annoying it must have been! Am I right in thinking that since you couldn't break our security measures your — er — outriders were deployed in scouring the country, hoping to get some clue concerning Gundersen's laboratory?'

'All possibilities had to be explored.'

'Including this part of Scotland, after months of futile effort. I'll say this for you, von Shroeder, you're a sticker.'

'Patience is invariably rewarded. One of my men became interested in this castle. Soon afterwards he disappeared. I received only one report from him. But it was enough! No more reports, no trace of him,' he said acridly. 'No cross on his grave, Herr Gayleigh!'

A low moan came through the open door, and a moment later the Russian who had been left with Gundersen appeared there. He caught von Shroeder's eye, nodded grimly, and turned back into the laboratory.

There was to be no more idle conversation, Peter gathered.

His ankles were untied, and he was told to get to his feet. Then the rope was bound round his arms as before.

'I should feel less like a captive bear if I had my shoes and socks,' he said, staring down at his feet.

'Since they cause more litter here Stefan will carry them for you,' was the sardonic reply.

He was urged forward to another door, finding it opened into the wide hall of the castle. A place of sombre silence with its stone floor, vaulted ceiling, and narrow windows. In earlier days it must have had all the bleakness of mediævalism, he thought. Now it had acquired a carpet, some rugs, and comparatively modern furniture.

Across the hall was a broad staircase flanked by dark panelling, and he was steered in this direction to a heavy door set with two massive iron bolts at the top and bottom. The ancient lock had evidently ceased to function, or was never used, for the door creaked open when the bolts were withdrawn.

Some stone steps led down under the staircase into impenetrable darkness, a dank, musty, odour coming up. Peter also detected a faint, rustling sound, his jaw tightening.

'Yes, you will not be alone,' von

Shroeder said significantly.

'You mean — ?'

'Rodents are not uncommon in old, disused wine cellars. But you will have other company.'

He switched on a naked light bulb at the head of the steps, which curved round, the cellar only coming into shadowy view when they had gone partly down.

Shirley Quentin was lying on the damp stone floor, her wrists bound behind her back to the rope securing her legs. And she was not the only one there.

A man, bound in the same way, was lying beside her.

Alan Sinclair.

Peter stiffened, an icy chill crawling down his spine. Sinclair — the one person he had been relying on to deal with this situation. And meanwhile Diana — ! How had they got Sinclair? Had it been at the house in Bridge of Allan?

The dread thought had barely flashed through his mind when von Shroeder's underling suddenly hurled his shoulder against him, sending him staggering headlong down the steps. Then his footwear was flung after him with a snarling epithet as he fell to his knees in the cellar.

Before he could get to his feet his captors had returned to the hall. The light was switched off, and the door creaked shut. The heavy bolts thudded home.

2

1

At the wheel of the big Jaguar Diana had by-passed Newark shortly after one o'clock. A brief halt for a cup of coffee and some chocolate to eat in the car, and she was on her way again driving hard along the A1.

Peter had stressed the urgency of this journey, and having failed to get through to him again on the phone she had hung up with very mixed feelings. Puzzlement, anxiety — and not a little annoyance. Without being given any explanation she was to drive up to Scotland as fast as possible to warn Sinclair. Four hundred odd miles!

Drop everything and start right away, he had virtually said, giving her no time to object.

Really! If it had been anyone but Peter . . .

A great deal must have happened since she had last seen him. He had mentioned something very hush-hush, extremely important, and he had expected to meet with opposition. Very dangerous opposition, apparently. Yet he had confided — if that was the word! — in no one but herself, before striding off in his cheerful, devil-may-care way. To what? She wished she knew, and with increasing anxiety, for the red light he took a delight in ignoring had been there again. During their many adventures together it had nearly always been so. But he was her man, and it was unthinkable that she should dismiss his urgent summons.

Once clear of London she had made good progress, her foot down hard on the accelerator, the Jaguar eating up the road.

Why hadn't Peter taken the car himself? Why had he gone by train? He had left before she had reached Jermyn Street, and Carver had been able to give her little information. Simply that a very attractive girl, a Miss Raeburn, had called that morning. After a short conversation, Peter had seen her into a taxi she had kept waiting, and had departed himself soon afterwards.

Who was this girl? According to Carver, he had seemed to know her quite well. How and where had he met her? Could it be that they were travelling together to Scotland? He had said nothing about her on the phone.

Apart from anything else this new friendship needed looking into, Diana thought, her pretty lips pursed. Yes, it would be interesting to meet this 'very attractive' girl. Whether they had left London together or not, it would seem she was very matey with Peter, because it was not the first time Carver had seen her. Peter had brought her back with him to Jermyn Street the previous night, and she had made a phone call before they had gone out again almost immediately afterwards, Peter having collected his tool-belt.

Where had they been going? The more Diana thought about it the more she was convinced this girl was involved in this very hush-hush business. Nay more, that something she knew had prompted his hurried departure for Scotland. Something she knew about Castle Dreich?

The Jaguar purred on, the speedometer needle touching 70 m.p.h. on clear stretches of road before she made Durham. A little further on she filled up with petrol, glad to stretch her legs before snatching some tea at a help-your-self café.

Then back behind the wheel again . . .

Newcastle with its quota of traffic. Some delay before she was through the town and heading north-west, speeding towards Edinburgh. Then finally the A9 to Falkirk and Stirling. Only a few miles now and she would be at Bridge of Allan and the end of her long, tiring journey.

The important message she was to deliver to Sinclair was brief in the extreme, she reflected. How would he react? Since Peter, as usual, had taken matters into his own hands without informing him, he would probably be extremely annoyed. And if he fired questions at her, as she foresaw he would, there was very little she could tell him. Moreover, as soon as she mentioned

Castle Dreich he would realise that she and Peter had abused his hospitality only a few days before.

No, all things considered she was not going to be very popular, she thought wryly. Peter had a lot to answer for.

A great deal more than she realised, for it never crossed her mind that Sinclair would not be there to receive her message.

It was shortly after 8 o'clock when she drove through Bridge of Allan, glimpsing the fir trees partly obscuring the house half a mile further on. The discordant cries of the crows she remembered so well had ceased now. With the setting sun casting red pennons across the sky they were settling down for the night.

Though it was still daylight shutters had been drawn over the windows, she saw as she pulled up outside. The old house had the appearance of being deserted. Or was Sinclair now taking more precautions? Locked windows would be no protection against a rifle bullet . . .

For the first time she felt a little nervous, glancing back over her shoulder as she went to the front door. But she saw nothing unusual. All was quiet.

The old-fashioned doorbell gave out its remote shuddering note as she pulled it. Then to her relief she heard the sound of footsteps in the hall. Thank goodness Sinclair was at home, she thought. He would be more than surprised to see her, without a doubt!

But the man who opened the door was someone she had never seen before. He was in his shirt sleeves, a youngish man with a broad flat face, his hair cut *en brosse*.

He looked at her inquiringly and when she said she would like to see Mr. Sinclair, motioned her in silently.

Diana stepped past him into the hall. Instantly the door was closed and relocked, but having been there before it didn't surprise her.

'I am Miss Caryll,' she said, wondering who the man was.

He merely stared at her. Evidently her name meant nothing to him.

'I'm a friend of Mr. Gayleigh's,' she added, rather impatiently. 'Where is Mr. Sinclair? I hope he's at home?'

The man nodded slowly, pointing silently towards the living-room, the menace in his gaze hidden from her as she hurried towards it, still unsuspiciously, but frowning slightly having already realised that neither Sinclair nor his housekeeper could be in there. Otherwise they would surely have shown themselves before now.

The house was very silent, she thought. Probably Mrs. Jamieson had gone out, yet surely Sinclair must have heard the front door bell. Why hadn't he appeared?

It was then she saw the leather motor-cyclist's jacket, tossed carelessly on to a divan!

Diana stiffened, staring at it. My God, this man who had admitted her . . .

She was swinging round with a rising sense of panic when a hand was clamped over her mouth. At the same moment a muscular arm went about her body and she was pushed violently forward to the door of the room Sinclair used as an office. The man opened it, half-pushing, half-carrying her inside as she struggled futilely in his powerful grip.

The room had been ransacked, and Mrs. Jamieson was in there, gagged and bound to a chair.

Von Shroeder's hireling jerked his hand away from Diana's mouth and before she could even cry out swept the edge of his palm down in a sharp, stunning blow on the back of her neck.

There must be no interference, and he knew his job.

Ten minutes later he was reporting over the scrambler phone to Castle Dreich.

2

'So they got you, too, Gayleigh!' Sinclair's strained voice came to him through the Stygian darkness of the cellar while he was still attempting to get to his feet. With his wrists bound tightly behind his back and his arms secured it was no easy matter. 'What the devil are *you* doing here?'

Peter said, breathing heavily: 'I was just about to ask you the same question.' He had his back against the damp wall now, his legs under him, prising himself slowly upright, the stone floor striking cold to his bare feet.

'Did you come alone?'

'Unfortunately, no. I might have done better if I had.'

'This is no time for riddles,' Sinclair retorted sharply. 'What do you mean by that?'

'I mean it's a long story. It can wait. When did they get their hands on you?'

An exclamation of frustration came back to him.

'Look, Gayleigh! Can't you answer a simple question? What Shirley and I want to know is whether you told anyone you were coming here. Did you?'

'None of your people — no. Only Diana.'

'Diana?'

'She's on her way now to your house. I expected you'd be there.'

There was a short pause. Then as Sinclair muttered bitterly: 'I was at my house when they came,' Peter felt a tightening of anxiety in his chest. He had been clinging to the faint hope that Diana wouldn't be driving into danger, that Sinclair had been with Gundersen at the castle when von Shroeder had taken possession of it.

'Three of 'em,' Sinclair went on. 'They got me while I was going to the garage this morning to — well, never mind why I went there — '

'To contact Gundersen, I suppose,' Peter put in, 'Oh yes, I know about your scrambler phone, and most of what's been going on up here and in London.'

'You do, eh?' Sinclair said with feeling. 'Why the devil couldn't you mind your own business?'

Peter said: 'Right now I'm worried about Diana. What happened after these three men sprang you?'

'After they'd finished with me I passed out,' was the gruff reply. 'The next thing I knew I was in the side-car of a motor-bike on the open moor, being driven here. Only two of them came back with me. Mrs. Jamieson was in the house, and God knows what's happened to her, poor woman! Now, it seems, you've dragged Diana into this mess. When will she get there?'

'Very soon now, I'm afraid,' Peter said quietly, feeling Sinclair's attitude towards him was fully justified. What Shirley Quentin was thinking he didn't know. So far she had said nothing. She had, he surmised, been kidnapped immediately after leaving Humphrey Maynard's house on the previous night. Since then she must have had a pretty rough time.

'Did you — did you see Professor Gundersen?' she said now, in a very distressed voice, and Peter hesitated before replying.

'Yes, I caught a glimpse of him.'

'What are they doing to him? Alan said he wouldn't tell them what they wanted to know. But that German chemist is quite unscrupulous and — '

It was Sinclair who interrupted quickly. Evidently he had seen, or realised, exactly what Gundersen would have to endure, but for Shirley's sake had played this subject down when she had raised it before.

'At least they haven't flung him into this black hole yet,' he said. 'That's not surprising, of course. He's their key piece. Since you claim to know so much, Gayleigh, I can tell you this. They won't find any notes, coded or otherwise, of his latest research. I know for a fact he's put nothing on paper. There's a model of the molecule he was working on in the laboratory, but it's not complete.'

Peter stared in his direction, wishing he could see his face. Because Sinclair, of course, had voiced only part of his thoughts, he knew that Gundersen had achieved a break-through only a few days before, even if his financée didn't, and all that it implied. Once von Shroeder got that vital information the final research on this deadly virus would be carried out in East German or Russian laboratories. And Gundersen would be grilled until he broke, as he soon would, however valiant he was.

Sinclair knew it. He must also know that after Gundersen had cracked he wouldn't be released. Not with the knowledge he possessed. Either he would be smuggled abroad, which would present difficulties, or he would be liquidated.

And it had been Sinclair's official responsibility to ensure that all went well at Castle Dreich. That he had failed in his duty, allowing himself to be caught off his guard at his house, must be adding to his bitterness now.

Peter said, on a brighter note: 'Well, since we're stuck in this place I think it's about time we made ourselves a little more comfortable, don't you? For one thing I'd like to put my socks and shoes on. This floor is hellishly cold.'

As an effort to relieve the tension, it failed lamentably. All Sinclair said was: 'Spare us your witticisms — please!'

'You misunderstand me,' Peter told him, a glint of accomplishment in his eyes. 'I don't profess to be an escapologist, but sometimes I can help myself a little — and others.'

He groped his way through the darkness towards the other two. Then as his foot encountered the man's body he halted. He knelt down, feeling with expert fingers for the knots in the rope that bound Sinclair.

At his touch Sinclair had stiffened. He had realised Gayleigh's hands must be free.

'Steady on, Alan. Loosen up. These knots are going to be tricky enough as it is.'

'But — ?'

'Yes, I know. You saw me trussed up. But I like to use my hands and arms when I can.' He was working on the rope fastening Sinclair's wrists now.

'Good for you, chum.' The change in Sinclair's voice was very noticeable. 'But how — ? My God, they bound *us* tightly enough!'

'Me too. Ease over a bit, will you? In the dark this is a bit dodgy.'

Shirley said, half eagerly, but as though unable to believe her ears. 'What are you doing? You don't mean — ?'

'This,' Sinclair muttered, 'is sheer wizardry. How did you manage it, Peter? Didn't they search you?'

'They searched me. Pretty thoroughly.'

'Well then?'

His strong fingers busy, Peter said: 'I've been frisked by objectionable characters before. Apart from looking in the obvious places they have a penchant for poking about in the innards of my clothes. *Ergo* I've learnt from sad experience to hide nothing there. But I always wear a ring on my little finger — as you may have noticed during our brighter moments together. It has a tiny built-in blade which can be released. I've found it very useful — particularly when the ungodly tie my hands behind my back.'

He hoped that didn't sound too clever, and he didn't say that with the ring held between his finger tips it had been far from easy to manœuvre the blade into position. One over eager movement and the ring might slip from his fingers on to the floor. In the dark that would have been a major catastrophe.

As it was he had been working away steadily as they talked, but not without some minor blood letting. There were quite a few cuts on his wrist where the small blade had bitten into his flesh instead of the rope. Nothing of any consequence, but he could feel the warm stickiness there now as he freed Sinclair, and then, with his assistance, the girl.

The other two had got stiffly to their feet when he said: 'You know this place better than I do. I couldn't see all of it from the steps. I suppose there isn't another door? No other way out?'

He was pretty sure what the answer would be before Sinclair said: 'Not a chance. Just solid stone walls.'

And the only door had looked as if it would withstand a battering ram, Peter recalled. Two massive bolts at the top and bottom. No, it would be impossible to force it open. That line of thought was definitely out. Even if it had been worth a try, hurling their shoulders against it, their efforts would, almost certainly, have been heard — and their gaolers had guns.

Nevertheless, Sinclair advanced it as a desperate possibility. 'If we could get one of von Shroeder's men to open the door we might overpower him,' he said hesitantly. 'It's a hell of a long shot, I admit.'

Peter said: 'You think he'd risk opening

it, if he was alone? I don't. From what I've seen of these men they use their heads. When he heard us kicking up a din why should he open the door at all? He'd know we couldn't get out. So would von Shroeder when it was reported to him. He could afford to laugh at our efforts. Our only advantage is that we can move about — and he doesn't know that yet. I feel we shouldn't let him know.'

'Then what do you suggest?' said Sinclair.

'Nothing very progressive, I'm afraid. But if they open that door unsuspectingly we shall have a much better chance. I'm thinking of Gundersen. It's just possible they might dump him in here.'

He didn't say: 'When they've broken him,' which he knew Sinclair would realise couldn't be long now. Meanwhile, they could do nothing to help him or themselves.

'Poor devil!' Sinclair muttered fiercely under his breath. 'Yes, I suppose it's worth a try. You stay down here, Shirley. 'I'll nip up to the top of the steps now.'

Peter said, with more optimism than he

felt: 'Right. I'll join you as soon as I've got my footgear on. I'll feel less like a monkey. Give me the wire if you hear anyone coming in the meantime.'

Five minutes later after groping about in the darkness he was more suitably clad. He went quietly up the cellar steps joining Sinclair behind the door.

All they could do now was wait.

4

It proved to be a long, fruitless wait. More than an hour had passed without an indication that Gundersen would be brought there. Nothing but silence. There had been no sign of anyone moving about in the hall. From time to time Shirley had joined them, for a whispered discussion, their hopes slowly fading. For all they knew von Shroeder and his men might already have left the castle, leaving them to their fate.

And Diana, Peter thought. By now, she must have reached Sinclair's house, and — Though he was not given to self-recrimination the thought hurt. Whatever had happened to her, he was responsible. He had been so damned clever, cockily sure that he could handle this without any assistance from Herrington! As it was, nobody knew of their predicament, nothing of what was happening at Castle Dreich. Ironically, he had gone out of his way to make sure of that!

As the minutes dragged by their whispered conversation had become fragmentary, their ears strained vainly for any sound beyond the door.

'Patience may be a virtue,' Sinclair muttered grimly, 'but I've a damned awful feeling this waiting business isn't going to work.'

Peter said, tight-lipped: 'No. It was just an idea.'

'The swine could have skipped by now, taking Gundersen with them. Obviously they wouldn't risk hanging around when they'd got what they wanted. They'd be off. Whether they've gone or not we can't go on playing this waiting game. You agree?'

'Yes.'

But the only alternative was to try conclusions with the door. A hundred years of tough, seasoned oak, secured by bolts! If Shroeder was still there and bothered to investigate he would be very much on his guard. Unarmed, there wasn't a chance in a million they could deal with him and his men. They might be even worse off than they were now, trussed up again.

It had to be faced.

And if he *had* gone? Then they could bang on the door with impunity — with precious little hope that anyone would hear them. Was it likely that anyone living on the moor would have ventured into the empty castle? It was not.

As yet, as a precaution, they had not switched on the light at the head of the cellar steps. Sinclair did that now, his strained, anxious gaze fixed on the door.

'Shoulder work first,' he said, through clenched teeth. 'Both of us together. At least, it's better than doing nothing.'

They drew back, then hurled themselves against it. It gave a creak, as if in derisive protest. Apart from that they might have been battling with a brick wall. And it was doubtful whether the sound it made would have carried beyond the wide hall.

They looked at each other. There was no need to speak.

'Again,' Sinclair said stubbornly.

The result was the same . . . and as they waited there was nothing to indicate their efforts had attracted any attention whatever.

Shirley was staring up at them anxiously from lower down the steps when suddenly they saw her tense, jerking her head back over her shoulder.

'What is it, Shirley?' Sinclair asked, frowning.

'I don't know. I — I thought I heard something. Yes, there it is again!'

Gayleigh and Sinclair heard it now. A faint scrabbling sound. It might have been a rat, or . . . It came from the wall of the cellar. The girl had turned back, disappearing round the bend in the steps when Sinclair said: 'Both of us can't go. You take a look-see, Peter.'

'Okay. Whistle if you want me.'

He went quickly down, catching up with the girl as she crossed to the far wall, pointing to it. They reached it together.

'Look!' she exclaimed excitedly.

A crack had appeared a few feet from the floor in the heavy stonework. And even as they stared at it, it became more noticeable, a small section of the wall moving fractionally. There could be no doubt now — somebody was trying to reach them.

Peter bent closer.

'Who's there?' he called out tensely. 'Can you hear me?'

There was no reply, and when he pressed hard with his shoulder against the stonework it didn't budge. Yet a moment later it moved again. Whoever was on the other side must be immensely strong.

A thought was flashing through his mind when Shirley said, her breath coming quickly with renewed hope: 'It must be! It can't be anyone else. When they brought you here did you see — ?'

'No, I didn't.' He knew what she meant.

Gregory!

He had been wondering what had happened to the man, but had assumed that von Shroeder had already dealt with him, either in the watch-tower, or elsewhere.

A distinct crevice was visible in the wall now, a block of stone more than two feet square being edged slowly back. A prodigious feat of strength, but this simple, deformed creature had carried a motor-bike bodily over the moor, Peter recalled, and —

He called out again, more vibrantly hoping for some faint response. There was none.

'Even if he can hear you, he can't answer,' Shirley said, breathing quickly. 'I mean Gregory — he's dumb. But he knew about the underground passage.'

'The passage?'

It was a relic of the rebellion of 1745, she told him, when the castle had been taken over by some of the Young Pretender's men.

'It's been blocked up for ages, of course. The other opening came out on to the moor. Gregory always found it fascinating. He could never keep away from it as a boy — '

'My God!' The interruption came from Sinclair. He had come partly down the cellar steps, staring across at them and at the wall. Shirley ran back towards him, and there was some tense discussion. Meanwhile Peter pressed hard against the stonework again. And now to some purpose. He felt it give.

The gap was slowly widening.

'Better get back to that door, Alan,' he breathed, using his shoulder again. 'I'll give Gregory all the help I can, but it's going to take time. I'll let you know what progress we're making.'

'Right,' Sinclair said, and was about to turn away when Shirley said: 'No I'll go. You help Peter.'

Even with his assistance it was slow work. Five minutes . . . ten minutes passed, both Gayleigh and Sinclair sweating with exertion. But the massive stonework had begun to yield more easily, though still very slowly. It had left an appreciable gap now, though there was still no sign of a breakthrough.

'Surely the damn wall can't be much thicker?' Sinclair panted.

'They built well in the old days,' Peter retorted, with equal frustration. 'Much too well! Let's keep at it, chum.'

The words were barely out of his mouth when Shirley came racing down the cellar steps, halting at the foot.

'Someone's coming,' she breathed. 'Quickly! The door!'

Both men stared at her in dismay — dismay all the more bitter since they had been so hopeful. Another few minutes and they might have escaped. As it was . . .

'Our original plan,' Peter gritted. 'There's nothing else for it.' A plan born of desperation, and with small hope of success. They had known that before, but now it had to be attempted.

'Quickly! Put out the light, Shirley.' This was Sinclair. He was already moving fast across the cellar together with Peter.

They reached her at the top of the steps only a few seconds after she had switched off the light. But precious seconds, for now they heard footsteps halt outside the door. Those of more than one man. It couldn't have been worse.

Then von Shroeder's voice, uttering an order in Russian.

A prayer on her lips, Shirley retreated down a few steps to give the two men more room. At the top there would be very little space for the work they had to do when the vital moment came.

Poised in readiness they heard one of the heavy bolts being drawn back. Then the other. The door creaked slowly open, spreading a patch of fading daylight coming in from the hall. Another few seconds and it would reveal all three of them, and in that short interval of time, before Gayleigh and Sinclair leapt forward, they saw that both the Russians were there, besides von Shroeder, the man called Ivan supporting the wretched pitiful object that was Professor Gundersen. He was dragging his legs, his eyes closed, and seemed to be delirious, every muscle in his body quivering.

'No more! . . . No more, for God's

sake!' they heard him cry. 'I'll tell you everything.'

Courageous as he had been, they had broken him.

Gayleigh went for the heavy-boned Stefan, taking him partly, but only partly, by surprise. The blow he unleashed at the man's chin merely glanced off it, his impetus carrying him past towards von Shroeder. Taken off his guard the big German couldn't draw his gun immediately, but as Peter cannoned into him, still off balance, thrust him back with an oath towards Stefan. He swung round smashing his fist into the man's stomach. A furious gasp, otherwise it made no impression.

Sinclair was having better luck with the other man. He had managed to get in several telling blows before the Russian rid himself of the Professor who crumpled on to the floor. But Sinclair's advantage was short lived. Von Shroeder had stepped back, his gun gripped firmly in his hand now.

Peter saw it. Not much time left! He swept his muscular arms round Stefan, pushing him back, through the door of the cellar. He cracked his head up against the broad jaw, drove a knee into the man's crutch. The Russian fell heavily against him, tripping him. Together they rolled down the gloomy steps past Shirley who did her best to help, kicking out hard at the man. It didn't stop him struggling until, momentarily on top of him, Peter seized his shoulders, smashing his head against the wall.

The man went limp. But too late. Up above, von Shroeder now had command of the situation. His gun barked, and Sinclair winced, clamping a hand to his forearm, the Russian grabbing him in a bear like grip.

There was nothing more Sinclair could do. It was almost the finish of an attempt which had been doomed to failure.

Von Shroeder said, with icy deliberation: 'There will be no more horseplay. Struggle, and you will get another bullet.'

Gayleigh couldn't see him, but the outcome of the brief battle in the hall was only too clear. He could retreat with Shirley down into the cellar, but that would merely delay the inevitable. They were beaten.

It was then he saw a faint halo of light moving exploringly over the wall near the dark bend in the stone stairway just behind him. At the same moment the girl saw it, too.

It could only be coming from a torch, both of them realising what it implied.

'Come on!' he panted, flinging an arm round her shoulder and darting with her down into the cellar. They had barely reached it when the light above them was snapped on, dimming the beam from the torch shining through the dark hole in the wall.

A hole just large enough for one of them to climb through with difficulty. Both of them couldn't possibly make it in time. One of them might.

'You first,' Peter said unhesitatingly.

'No!' She was hanging back.

'*Come on!*'

'No, it's better you go. I'm staying with Alan. Alone, you might have a chance.'

'To hell with that!'

'But don't you *see*,' she implored

bravely. '*You* must go. It's our only hope. Don't argue — *please!'*

Since she was adamant he had no choice, unless he stayed with her which would have gained them nothing. Somehow he had to get help before von Shroeder could use the vital information he had extracted from Gundersen.

He shot her a glance full of admiration, then bounded on to the gap in the wall, the torchlight almost blinding him now. He couldn't see Gregory, but felt the roughness of a woollen sweater against his face as a powerful arm seized him, jerking him forward. The man had heard Shirley's frantic exhortation, and evidently understood.

Von Shroeder had almost reached the bottom of the steps, a bullet biting into the wall within an inch of the hole, when Peter felt himself pulled, as if he had been as light as a child, into the gloom of the tunnel.

He had fallen on his face, and was picking himself up breathlessly, when his rescuer squatted down, heaving up the huge lump of stone he had dislodged. He staggered forward with it, ramming it back into place, uttering a grunt of exultant accomplishment. Neither von Shroeder nor his bullets could reach them now. Temporarily, he was thwarted.

The tunnel was in a surprisingly good state of preservation, Peter saw, as the bow-legged, ape-like man snatched up the torch and pushed past him, beckoning. Though in places the roof had collapsed, the blackened wood supporting it damp and rotten with age, he found there was always room to scramble through. Gregory's work, perhaps earlier that long day? It must have been, he thought.

The muddy ground sloped steadily upwards, and after making their way slowly along it for almost a hundred yards, they came to the entrance. It had been hidden by a large, flat stone covered with earth and grass-grown, lying in the side of a hillock.

Peter emerged into the mist-ridden twilight of oncoming night, his raincoat and suit a muddy wreck, his hands slimy with earth as he breathed in the moorland air thankfully, filling his lungs with it.

They had come out at the back of the castle. It loomed large and sinister. But there was no sign of von Shroeder or his cohorts. Not yet. There would be very soon!

His keen eyes surveyed the desolate expanse of moorland, then switched to his even more bedraggled rescuer. In the half-light he looked more ape-like than ever, his bare feet thick with mud, his unprepossessing face unshaven, showing a growth of coarse, dark stubble. But this loyal creature was far from an ape — he was a man.

'Thanks,' Peter said. 'Now you'd better come along with me.'

But he shook his head, unintelligible sounds coming from his lips, gesticulating with vehement earnestness. He jabbed a thick finger at Peter, and towards the moor. Then he struck his barrel-shaped chest, pointing to Castle Dreich, and set off back there with his peculiar rolling gait, muttering inarticulately.

Peter didn't try to stop him. If any man knew his way around those parts it was Gregory, he thought. And despite his appearance he wasn't simple. A staunch ally.

Swiftly he considered possibilities. The motor-cycles he had seen were invisible from this point. He could try to make his get-away on one of them, but there was little hope that he could manage it without being seen. He couldn't afford to take that risk, yet he would be at a grave disadvantage on foot when the hunt began.

It was a grim prospect. But there was no alternative.

Only seconds after Gregory had left him he was racing across the open moor.

3

1

The rocky summit of the hill from which he had obtained his first glimpse of Castle Dreich with Diana was less than half a mile away. He headed in that direction, across the broad end of the valley, crouching low as he ran. In the far distance was Strathyre. It seemed a million miles away. For he had not covered more than a couple of hundred yards when a rifle bullet whined past him.

He swerved, narrowly avoiding another, then flung himself to the ground, crawling feverishly through a patch of heather to a small hillock which would provide a temporary shield. Before he reached it, scrambling round it, more shots had followed him.

He plunged on, thankful for the deepening twilight, and the start the outlet to the tunnel had given him. The shots were coming from a point much nearer the castle. He had that slight advantage, and since von Shroeder and the two Russians were all heavily built men he was pretty sure he could outdistance them on foot — if he didn't take a bullet! He began to regulate his breathing settling down to a steady stride.

The rifle fire had ceased, the castle more than a third of a mile behind him when he caught the sound of a motorbike starting up. Then another. Just as he had feared. The pursuit was being organised now. He was rapidly approaching the rocky hill which had been his objective. He had hoped to skirt it, and use it for cover, racing straight on. But that would be courting disaster with a motor-bike after him and since they had seen him heading that way. He had to change his direction, otherwise in a very few minutes — He veered off to the left of the hill, covered another hundred yards, then flattened himself on the ground.

By then he had seen the misty headlight coming closer, and heard the note of another motor-bike. Two of them to contend with now! The first one was coming on fast, but to his infinite relief it turned to the right when it reached the hill, disappearing round it. A minute later the second rider came up, taking the same route.

Pretty soon they would realise he had stopped running and was hiding somewhere. But if they thought he had got beyond the hill they would begin searching that part of the moor. He hoped so most fervently as he got to his feet, dashing on, his lips tightly compressed, for his change of direction meant he had a greater distance to cover. Maybe a couple of miles more than before, since he was now heading towards the lower end of Loch Lubnaig. The odds were piling up against him.

Then to add to his anxiety he saw something that resembled a large bird superimposed against the indistinct outline of the castle.

The helicopter!

It must, he realised, have been housed beyond the wall at the far end of the laboratory, the machine in which Gundersen had brought Sinclair to confer with him at Castle Dreich, to deal with the situation created by Gregory and the body in the loch. An emergency — now it was being used again, in very different hands! An additional menace, since it was still light enough for him to be spotted more easily from the air.

It came flying low. Crouching on the moor, he watched it over his shoulder, sweating. It reached the hill he had avoided, gained altitude slightly, flew over it, and disappeared.

Reprieve! It must have turned away to the right.

The more time he could gain the better. It would mean they would have to search a wider area, also it was getting slowly darker. On again. He had covered another quarter of a mile before the helicopter came back into sight.

And now, he saw, it was coming straight in his direction, like a huge malignant vulture. Would it change course before it reached him? It did, very slightly, and at that moment, lying on his face, he thanked God for the raincoat he was wearing. It's fawn colour would be almost indistinguishable from the surrounding ground — helped by a little camouflage. He had wormed his way into some more heather, tearing some of it up to partly cover him.

The machine flew past within twenty yards of the spot where he was lying, Corinne Raeburn in the driving-seat. Among her other accomplishments she was a qualified pilot, he recalled. There were very few sports at which she didn't excel, and this one, the cruel intention behind it, must be right up her street. The cat and mouse game.

Soon after she had passed him she swung the machine round, flying back and into the near distance before returning again and again, but covering the ground farther away from him. Evidently she thought he must have got farther north, in the direction of Strathyre.

As soon as he dared he was on the move again, but slower now, his heart pounding against his ribs with exertion.

To his right he could see the foraging beams of the two motor-cycles. The search was widening. It wouldn't be long before he was cut off even from the lengthier route he was taking.

The helicopter had receded into the distance, almost invisible in the darkening sky, when he saw that it was returning to the castle. Apparently defeated by the fading light. From the air, lying motionless, he would have been very difficult to locate now. The realisation gave him new hope — quickly dispelled when he saw twin headlights away to his left. The Morris. Reinforcements. And he had the sickening thought that as soon as the girl got back the third motor-cycle with the sidecar would be brought into use.

They certainly meant business. And though he refused to dwell on it, he knew that it was only a matter of time before they would be able to encircle him, pressing in.

The Morris was coming straight towards him, driving fast along the only semblance of a road leading from the castle. He had seen this road for the first time before setting off, but had deliberately avoided it.

Down on the ground again.

A couple of minute later the Morris was still continuing along the rough track, which had veered away to his left a couple of hundred yards away now. Soon it would drive past him. But it had barely done so when it turned off to the right, came on, and to his increasing consternation halted not more than fifty paces ahead of him. His eyes glued to it, he saw Eidervik step out on to the moor, a gun in his hand. Then he leaned back into the car for something.

A torch!

He flashed it around, the extremity of the pale fan of light passing wanly over his quarry. But again the raincoat Peter had longed to discard as he ran served him well. Eidervik hadn't seen him yet, though if the man took a few steps forward —

He didn't. He went round the other side of the car, walking farther away from it, flashing the light around there. Never slow to miss an opportunity Peter's eyes gleamed.

He moved silently up to the Morris, crouching as he ran, reaching it while Eidervik was still searching the ground beyond, his back towards him. The car door had been left wide open, the engine ticking over. But to have sprung into the driving-seat and driven off would have been fatal. If he had managed to avoid a bullet, the two motor-cyclists would have been instantly alerted. They could have headed him off, travelling much faster than the Morris.

So, first, he had to eliminate Eidervik.

He insinuated himself into the car, still crouching, tilted the passenger seat forward very quietly, and crept round to the back. It was no easy matter, and there was the constant fear that the Norwegian would return before he was ready for him.

But his luck was in. He heard the man's heavy tread, felt the small car lurch as Eidervik lowered himself into the driving-seat. And he had barely done so when Peter's arm fastened round the fleshy neck. There was a quickly stifled yelp, and it might have been all over in a matter of seconds.

But the Norwegian was stronger than he had imagined. Writhing and twisting he fell through the open door of the car, Peter still retaining his grip dragging himself over the driving-seat after him, struggling to reach the gun still in the man's hand. On the ground he finally managed to get his knee on Eidervik's outstretched arm. Then releasing his grip, tore the gun away with both hands from his fingers, smashing it down with stunning force on to his head. Ten seconds later he was back in the car and moving away, gasping.

It had been a damn near thing, he thought. If Eidervik had managed to fire just one shot, or even cry out — As it was, the two other searchers couldn't know what had happened.

He swung the car round, driving back to the cart-track of a road, as Eidervik might have done, the headlights still on. Then he zig-zagged away from it and back again repeatedly, as if searching, moving slowly but steadily farther and farther away from danger.

With grim satisfaction he saw these tactics were paying off. The motor cyclists took no notice of him, still quartering the ground in the increasing distance. The nearest man was almost a mile away when he switched off the car lights, pressing down harder on the accelerator. A little more time gained. He would make it. They couldn't overtake him now.

Some ten minutes later he reached the Pass of Leny below Loch Lubnaig. The main road. There had been a belated attempt at pursuit, soon abandoned. Clear of the moor he could travel much faster, his immediate concern for Diana . . .

Bridge of Allan.

Another twenty minutes hard driving and he pulled up sharply outside the police station there. He strode inside, his eyes steely with purpose. The inspector in charge was speaking to the desk-sergeant as he confronted them, an unkempt but commanding figure.

'My name is Peter Gayleigh. I have a matter of the utmost importance to report . . . '

2

The inspector had moved fast, contacting County Headquarters at Perth. By now the Dunblane and Crieff subdivisions had been alerted, police on their way to Castle Dreich. But whether they would get there before von Shroeder had gone was most unlikely, Peter thought. He wouldn't have wasted any time.

What had happened to Sinclair and Shirley Quentin? He wished he knew. But uppermost in his mind was Diana. What had happened to *her*? There could be no doubt she had reached Sinclair's house, for as he hurried towards it together with the inspector and two constables, he saw his Jaguar standing outside, his mouth tightening with anxiety.

'Better I go first,' he said crisply. And as he saw the inspector was about to demur: 'Listen. You're wearing uniforms. I'm not. When this man realises the police are after him he's liable to give a lot of trouble before you nab him. But he doesn't know me. I could be any visitor from the village.'

By now he had spruced himself up a little. The inspector saw his point, rubbing his chin.

'You think you can get him to open the door?'

'I can try, if you and your men keep out of sight. I suggest you send one of them round to the back.'

'Very well.'

Half a minute later Peter reached the gate. He opened it, and in case he had already been seen, walked unhurriedly up the short garden path before pulling at the doorbell.

There was no answer. He rang again, after waiting for a while. Still no reply. Undeterred, hoping to convey the impression that he knew someone must be in, he rang a third, fourth, and fifth time, pretty certain he had been seen — seen to be alone.

Still, he waited, and presently he heard muffled footsteps in the hall. The man must have realised his visitor had no intention of leaving. The bolts were drawn, the lock turned. Then the door was opened a few inches.

'Ah!' Peter's exclamation merely suggested rewarded persistence. 'I've called to see Mrs. Jamieson. I wonder if — ?'

His shoulder smashed against the door. At the same instant he reached for the gun he had taken from Eidervik. Then he was in the hall, the man staggering back. Peter leapt after him, jabbing the muzzle into his stomach.

'Hold it, bud — or you'll hold a bullet!' His eyes were like ice. 'Now talk. Where is she?'

The man stiffened, then as he saw the police officers striding up the path, cringed farther back. Very ungentle hands had seized him when he pointed towards the livingroom door.

Peter strode in there, glanced swiftly around, saw the closed door facing him, the key in the lock. In seconds he had it open, finding Diana and the older woman gagged and bound.

★ ★ ★

'You were a long time in coming,' Diana said, Peter's arm about her after she and

286

Mrs. Jamieson had been released.

'I was delayed somewhat, darling. I'm sorry. Damned sorry. I think I can guess what happened. That swine — ! How do you feel now?'

'Much better,' she told him wryly.

'I'll get you a drink.'

She nodded. 'After that gag I could certainly do with one — Mrs. Jamieson, too, I'm sure.'

'Aye, I wouldn't mind.'

Though she had been badly shaken by her experience she wasn't going to admit it. Mrs. Jamieson was made of stern stuff.

While the police attended to the removal of their captive Diana gave Peter a brief account of what had occurred. The man had been led away by the two constables when the inspector returned to get further particulars.

It was then Peter said purposefully: 'There's a telephone in the garage. Excuse me, I'll be back in a minute.'

'Now look, sir!' the inspector frowned. 'This is a matter for — ' But his words fell on thin air. Peter had gone.

In the garage he picked up the

telephone book, found the number of Castle Dreich. Would he get an answer? He might, if von Shroeder had left, and — Anxiously, he called the number.

He heard the ringing note — then Sinclair's voice.

'Alan! Peter here.'

Sinclair said: 'Good man! I heard you'd made it. The police called me. Where are you speaking from?'

'From your place. I've been giving the local cops a hand.'

'Diana and Mrs. Jamieson?'

'Yes. They're both here, quite safe now. Your unwanted tenant didn't give much trouble. How about von Shroeder,' he hurried on. 'He's scarpered, I take it?'

'Huh-huh, more than half an hour ago. Gregory released Shirley and me after the whole tribe had left.'

Von Shroeder and the Raeburn girl in the helicopter, Peter thought grimly. Maybe Eidervik as well. By now it would be miles away, well clear of pursuit, a mere speck in the dark sky.

'But von Shroeder won't get far,' Sinclair was saying with keen satisfaction.

'Thanks to Gregory. We owe a lot to him — he put the chopper out of action, Peter.'

'What? The helicopter?'

'I'm telling you. He sneaked up to it in the dark while it was standing outside the castle. Did they use it to go after you?'

'Yes.'

'I thought so. It must have just got back when Gregory got at it. Nobody was in sight when he did his stuff — I guess you were keeping 'em all pretty busy! And that isn't all he did. Some time later he got at the engine of a motor-bike with a side-car, and fixed it — after the two Russians had scarpered. I've no doubt von Shroeder, together with another man and a girl I didn't know were there, meant to make their getaway in the chopper. Gregory put paid to that! But he took a bullet in the leg from this bitch of a girl while he was slipping away after fixing the motor-bike. Shirley is attending to him and the Professor now.'

Peter was gripping the phone tighter. 'You're telling me von Shroeder and these other two had to leave on foot?'

'Just that. They hadn't any choice.'

'My God, Alan!'

'Exactly. By the time they found the chopper had been got at, the other two men had already gone. I tell you, Peter, Gregory deserves a medal. Von Shroeder can't have got clear of the moor. I'd have gone after him myself, but he winged me during the scrap in the hall. Nothing serious. I'll live.' There was a brief pause, then: 'Ah, the cops are here! Be seeing you.'

Peter hung up, his thoughts switching to his Jaguar parked outside the house. The temptation to drive off right away to what promised to be the showdown was strong. But there had always been times in his chequered career when the authority of the police could not be discounted. That, and their means of communication. Alone on the vastness of the moor, if he was permitted to get that far, it was unlikely he would be in at the finish without their co-operation.

The local inspector must be brought abreast of developments. Then if he had any blood in his veins . . .

Back in the house he imparted his

latest information, the inspector listening keenly, Diana and Mrs. Jamieson with complete mystification.

'My car's just outside,' Peter reminded him. 'It's only a few miles to Dunblane. They'll be getting more news through there.'

The inspector looked at him keenly.

'Very well, Mr. Gayleigh,' he said crisply.

3

The sergeant in charge at the Dunblane station was being kept fully informed of developments, men from his section having gone to take part in the operation. Police were now converging on the moor from all points. Already, the two motor-cyclists had been intercepted on the road between Comrie and Crieff, trapped by a road block which had been set up very promptly.

At the inspector's elbow, Peter said: 'Just small fry. It's von Shroeder we want!'

Sinclair would have made that very clear, he thought. And probably by now he was in one of the police cars, joining in the hunt. At Dunblane they could only wait, since von Shroeder had not been sighted yet and could have made off in any direction.

The minutes dragged slowly by . . .

'If he headed due west to the nearest main road we should have nabbed him by now,' the inspector said fretfully.

Peter nodded. 'If I know von Shroeder he won't have done. More likely he's gone to ground.'

'Hoping to slip through our net in the dark, you mean . . . H'mm.'

It was a nerve racking possibility, since it would have needed an army of police to cover the moor thoroughly. How many of them had been issued with guns? Very few, Peter imagined. And von Shroeder and the girl were both armed, as he knew to his cost, probably Eidervik, too, since he had evidently managed to get back to the castle.

'Another report coming through, sir,' the sergeant intimated suddenly, his ear glued to the telephone connecting him with Southern Division headquarters.

'Well?' the inspector asked impatiently.

'Radio message received from a patrol car, sir.' He listened for a few moments, then: 'They've been located — two men and a woman!'

'Where?'

'Half a mile south of Ben Vorlich, sir.'

'Good!'

'Superintendent Munro is on his way there now, sir.'

Peter had already swung round on his heel, and was striding out to the Jaguar when the inspector followed him keenly. He was attached to the Stirlingshire Constabulary and this was a Perthshire operation, but he wasn't going to miss it.

Doune . . . Callender . . . and on to Strathyre. Very familiar with this route, the speed limit ignored, Peter covered it in less than a quarter of an hour. Without officialdom at his side it would have been very different, he thought, as they passed vigilant police officers. A further sign to a constable stationed on the fringe of the moor at Strathyre, and they were travelling across it along a track the inspector pointed out.

Very much slower now, but faster than the previous journey Peter had made in the Morris. The big car bucketed and swayed, plunging forward, the darkness dissipated by the powerful headlights.

He was fully preoccupied with driving when he felt a touch on his arm.

'Over there,' his passenger said, pointing to a cluster of light in the distance, away to their left.

'Okay!'

A few minutes later they came up to the stationary police cars. They were standing at a very respectful distance from a large boulder at the foot of a steep hill, Ben Vorlich looming up like a dark cloud not very far beyond. The cars had spread out, providing a shield for the police officers gathered behind them. The reason was very soon plain, for as the Jaguar approached a bullet screamed past the radiator.

It could only have come from a rifle — and from the direction of the boulder.

Peter saw Sinclair, his left arm in a

sling, speaking to a man who seemed to be in authority. Superintendent Munro. He waved them round behind the other cars, in no uncertain way. As the Jaguar pulled up the inspector hastened towards him, Sinclair meeting Peter as he stepped out.

'So you wanted to be in at the finale,' he said, grimly. 'Same here. We've got 'em pinned down, but there are difficulties.'

'So I see.'

'Besides the rifle they've got three pistols — plugged one of the police chaps in the leg already. He crawled too close and this bitch of a girl got him. She's a bloody good shot. Who the hell is she?'

Peter said. 'No one you know. I think you'll be more interested in the man with von Shroeder. I'd have mentioned him before, but we had other things on our mind in that cellar. Shirley saw him quite often — Osvald Eidervik.'

Sinclair blinked.

'Eidervik! But — My God you don't mean — ?'

' 'Fraid so, Alan. Your trusted boffin! He's been in von Shroeder's pay almost from the beginning of this lark. I'll tell you about it sometime. Not now.'

A burst of shots rang out from the hill, and for an instant the head and shoulders of one of the advance party was visible, silhouetted in the wan moonlight. He darted farther back. Evidently he had narrowly escaped being hit, yet he had been barely within range of the pistol bullets.

Almost another casualty. The Superintendent had seen it, his mouth tightening. His was the responsibility.

'How many men has he got out there?' Peter asked.

'Only half a dozen now,' Sinclair told him. ' I don't envy 'em. If they get close enough to do their stuff it'll be a miracle.'

'You've tried taking them from the rear, I suppose?'

'You bet. That's how we got our casualty. There are more of our chaps on the far side of the hill, of course.'

Faced with the continuing risk to his men the superintendent had made a decision.

'Can't go on like this,' Munro said

grimly to one of the officers at his side. 'Get on the talk-back to Inspector Duncan. All personnel to cease further approach.' Duncan was in charge of the contingent Sinclair had mentioned. 'I'll speak to our men out here. Hand me that megaphone.'

'Maybe we'll have to wait until first light, sir.'

'Maybe. Get busy.'

His amplified voice was carrying over the moor when Peter Gayleigh moved quietly away. These instructions applied to the police, and he didn't happen to be one of them. Moreover, in such close proximity to officialdom he invariably felt constrained, a heritage of his less regenerate days. His arrival there had been facilitated by the inspector. But it was now time, he felt, to do some prospecting on his own account.

He moved farther back into the gloom, all lights from the police cars having been extinguished soon after he had seen them in the distance from the Jaguar. Opposed by rifle fire, due precautions had been taken.

His own car was also in darkness, serving to shield his silent departure. As yet Sinclair hadn't noticed he had slipped away, and nobody else was taking any interest in him, all eyes focused in the opposite direction across the moor. By the time he was missed — He quickened his steps, crouching low as he took a wide circuitous route which would eventually bring him much closer to the opposition.

It took him nearly a quarter of an hour before he reached a point away to the right of the boulder and almost within pistol range of it.

It also brought him to a constable, lying flat in the heather, a revolver in his hand.

Peter said, in a whisper: 'Stay where you are, chum,' and went on, wriggling forward on his stomach now. Not towards the boulder. His immediate objective was the side of the hill some fifty yards away. As yet he hadn't attracted any fire, having taken advantage of a sullen cloud obscuring the moon. But soon it would emerge again shedding its ghostly light.

Before it did, he must reach the shadow cast by some overhanging rock he had detected on the slope of the hill. And he thought he could make out the semblance of a gully running past that spot.

After edging forward another ten yards he was pretty sure this shallow depression had been carved out by a stream at some time. It appeared to have dried up now, since he could detect no sound of trickling water, and sloped slightly upwards on his left. Could he get there before the moon defeated him, revealing his position? His jaw tight, he glanced up at the dark sky. He had a couple of minutes, he reckoned, no more.

At that moment a bullet bit into the ground just in front of him, the powder flash coming from the boulder. He froze, flat on his stomach, holding his breath.

But the bullet was followed by others, progressively farther away to his left, some of them much farther away. He realised he hadn't been seen. Shots fired at random, to deter any furtive approach. Very obviously von Shroeder and Co. were not short of ammunition!

He reached the overhang and the gully only a few seconds before the moon rode out, turning the darkness into a misty grey almost as impenetrable. The bed of the stream was damp, but not wet, for which he was thankful as he began to creep along it away from the shadow of the rock, edging forward inch by inch.

He had covered another twenty yards laboriously when another barrage of shots sounded below him. Apparently they had been aimed in approximately the same directions as before and with no particular mark in view.

It puzzled him a little, suggesting that the opposition was becoming rather panicky. Not von Shroeder surely? *His* nerve wouldn't crack. He was a hardened ex-Himmler man, the type who would wait, ready to pick off any of his adversaries with deliberate precision. It was surprising he had allowed such pointless shooting.

Gayleigh raised himself cautiously on his elbows, risking a reconnoitring glance. He saw the boulder obliquely ahead and slightly below him, and two indistinct figures crouching behind it. Only two. The fleshy bulk of Eidervik and the girl.

From her savage attitude she appeared to be trying to restrain him from wasting more ammunition.

Where was von Shroeder?

There was no sign of the man as Gayleigh screwed up his eyes endeavouring to pierce the darkness farther away, his very alert gaze ranging over the hillside. Nothing stirred there.

He waited for a time, hidden by the gully, raising his head more than once, stealing further wary glances around. Still nothing. Then suddenly he heard the report of a rifle way above him. No bullet. It seemed to have been fired in the opposite direction, away from the hill. Which could only mean one thing. Von Shroeder had climbed up to the dark summit to deal with any advance of the police stationed on the far side.

Gayleigh continued his slow progress, a steely light in his eyes. Another five minutes and he was above the boulder and less than twenty yards away from it. The time was now ripe for action, his only regret that he hadn't his Walther.

Eidervik's automatic would have to suffice.

He raised himself on his elbows again, taking careful aim. Then very deliberately he squeezed the trigger. The other two had their backs towards him, the bullet chipping away a fragment of stone less than a foot above the Norwegian's head.

'All right, boys, we've got 'em,' he called out, as if backed by a police party. And louder: 'Drop those guns!'

He had ducked down as Eidervik and the girl jerked round in alarm. Corinne Raeburn's pistol spat viciously but harmlessly in his direction. Eidervik's mouth was agape with fright. For a moment the man seemed to be paralysed. Then before she could fire again he swept her in front of him, edging sideways.

Peter's bullet, aimed at Eidervik's gun arm, found another mark. The girl gave a gasp, clutching at her breast, her brave ally crying out shrilly: 'Don't shoot! Don't shoot, for God's sake!' And he continued to shield himself behind her, dropping his own gun.

Then as he realised she had been hit he

released her, darting away with frantic haste round the boulder and out of sight.

The girl had collapsed on to the ground, motionless, when Gayleigh crept warily down to her. She might still be dangerous, her pistol still in her hand. But she didn't move as he drew closer, lying partly on her side. He frowned, and had almost reached her when he saw that her eyes were wide open, staring expressionlessly into the night.

Corinne Raeburn! Only a short while ago she had been vitally alive, viciously asserting her independence to the last. He shook his head with a sigh. She had lived as she had died, wildly, and he could summon up little remorse. She would have shot him without compunction, given the chance, if events had turned out differently.

As for Eidervik — He had come into view again, stumbling across the moor towards the police cars. He had taken something from his pocket, a handkerchief it seemed, waving it frantically in surrender, and calling out as he ran. Peter's lips curled. No need to go after him. In any case it would have been foolish, for he was reminded very forcibly of von Shroeder as a rifle bullet whined past him.

There was nothing craven about this final adversary. He would resist to the last, even if he thought a police party was down below, coming for him. Very soon they would arrive, but Peter Gayleigh didn't wait for them. He shifted his position quickly, began to weave his way up the dark hill.

It wasn't very high and from the rifle report he was pretty certain his quarry had crept a little way down from the summit. He must now be within range of small arms fire, but Gayleigh didn't attempt to use his own gun yet. Instead, he picked up some small stones from the sparse, coarse grass, tossing them well away to right and left of him, fostering the impression that he was far from alone.

It brought no response from von Shroeder. Even if he thought he was outnumbered he wasn't going to fire again, revealing where he was concealed, until he could pick off something tangible.

Gayleigh was no longer in direct line with the boulder, having moved round at an angle, his narrowed gaze seeking for the faintest indication of a crouching silhouette. And presently he saw it, an amorphous patch of retreating darkness. His ruse had evidently been successful, for von Shroeder was edging back to the summit. If he had known he was being tracked by one man alone he would never have given ground.

In the distance the muted sound of official voices was audible, growing fainter, implying that Eidervik had found his unhappy haven and was being escorted away. Glancing back, Peter caught a glimpse of a dark shadow, one of many, he surmised, now at the foot of the hill. The police were closing in.

He climbed up another few yards, keeping the slowly retreating figure within range. Near the crest of the hill the ground rose more steeply. Von Shroeder couldn't continue to back away without turning round. To reach the far side he would be obliged to expose himself more. His gun at the ready, Peter waited grimly for the moment when his quarry attempted this desperate manœuvre.

He hadn't long to wait — and as soon as the bulky outline of the German showed, he fired.

His target slid a few inches down the hill, something slipping from his grasp. From the sound it made as it slithered down the slope it could have been the rifle. But if he had been hit, he recovered quickly, almost flinging himself forward over the crest. The next instant a pistol bullet scudded into the ground near Gayleigh.

Wounded or not, the man was dangerous, still armed.

Peter changed his position silently, then began to creep forward again with cool determination. He could hear others moving behind him now. So, apparently, could von Shroeder. He fired once more, then vanished. Very soon he would also have to contend with Inspector Duncan's men. By now, he must be bitterly aware that he was closely hemmed in from all sides, the information he had extorted from Gundersen of no use to him.

Gayleigh was still some distance away to the left when he decided to risk a swifter approach. He had darted to his feet, half-running, half-scrambling to the top of the hill when he saw von Shroeder again. Contemptuous of taking further cover, the man was now standing upright, his left arm hanging limp. His right arm was bent, his gun pointing to his head. The ignomy of capture was not for the Herr Doktor Ulrich von Shroeder.

There was a muffled report. Then he staggered forward a few steps before collapsing, a bullet in his brain . . .

★　★　★

'There are still a few things I can't figure out,' Sinclair said, sitting with Peter in the back of one of the police cars. 'I gather you knew this Raeburn girl.'

'Only slightly, Alan. When I first met her she had me pinned against a wall, taking pot shots at me.' Their brief association had ended much in the same way as it had begun, he thought. With violence. But with all her faults she had not lacked courage. 'I'd rather not talk about her just now. I've never shot a woman before.'

'We all realise how it happened, Peter.'

'Yes, even so . . . '

They were on their way back to Castle Dreich, the police cars having dispersed, Superintendent Munro accompanying Eidervik in one of them, another employed as a hearse.

Presently, Sinclair said: 'You never told me how you got into this thing in the first instance. It was supposed to be top secret. Who put you wise?'

Herrington!

Peter said, thinking hard: 'I'm glad you asked me that question. But it isn't easy to answer.' (By heaven, it wasn't, since at one time Sinclair himself, among others, had been suspected of leaking information.) 'To cut a long story short it was largely a matter of deduction, after I got tangled up with Corinne Raeburn. She knew your Shirley was acting as a messenger since she was in cahoots with Eidervik and von Shroeder. I simply muscled in on my own account — sheer curiosity,' he added quickly.

'H'm.' Sinclair looked at him. 'You mean you'd met the girl before you visited me at Bridge of Allan.'

'Er — yes. Some time before.'

Nobody could refute it, except Eidervik. Let others sort that out, including Herrington and his superiors. They had thought fit to employ him, and he had done his best, even if he hadn't co-operated as they might have wished.

He had a distinct feeling that Herrington might have quite a lot to say to him when they next met . . .

THE END

We do hope that you have enjoyed reading this large print book.

Did you know that all of our titles are available for purchase?

We publish a wide range of high quality large print books including:
Romances, Mysteries, Classics
General Fiction
Non Fiction and Westerns

Special interest titles available in large print are:
The Little Oxford Dictionary
Music Book, Song Book
Hymn Book, Service Book

Also available from us courtesy of Oxford University Press:
Young Readers' Dictionary
(large print edition)
Young Readers' Thesaurus
(large print edition)

For further information or a free brochure, please contact us at:
Ulverscroft Large Print Books Ltd.,
The Green, Bradgate Road, Anstey,
Leicester, LE7 7FU, England.
Tel: (00 44) **0116 236 4325**
Fax: (00 44) **0116 234 0205**

Other titles in the
Linford Mystery Library:

DEATH CALLED AT NIGHT

R. A. Bennett

Jimmy Ellis believes his parents have died in a car crash when as a young boy he is taken to live with relatives in Australia. The years pass happily, then the nightmare comes. Terrifying images flit through his mind in the dark — all through the eyes of a child, a witness to grisly events seventeen years before. He begins to delve into the past, and soon he finds himself on the trail of a double murderer — a murderer who is prepared to kill again.

THE DEAD TALE-TELLERS

John Newton Chance

Jonathan Blake always kept appointments. He had kept many, in all sorts of places, at all sorts of times, but never one like that one he kept in the house in the woods in the fading light of an October day. It seemed a perfect, peaceful place to visit and perhaps take tea and muffins round the fire. But at this appointment his footsteps dragged, for he knew that inside the house the men with whom he had that date were already dead . . .

THREE DAYS TO LIVE

Robert Charles

Mike Harrigan was scar-faced, a drifter, and something of a woman-hater. With his partner Dan Barton he searched the upper reaches of the Rio Negro in the treacherous rain forests of Brazil, lured by a fortune in uncut emeralds. Behind them rode three killers who believed that they had already found the precious stones. And then fate handed Harrigan not emeralds, but the lives of women, three of them nuns, and trapped them all in a vast series of underground caverns.

TURN DOWN AN EMPTY GLASS

Basil Copper

L.A. private detective Mike Faraday is plunged into a bizarre web of Haitian voodoo and murder when the beautiful singer Jenny Lundquist comes to him in fear for her life. Staked out at the lonely Obelisk Point, Mike sees the sinister Legba, the voodoo god of the crossroads, with his cane and straw sack. But Mike discovers that beneath the superstition and an apparently motiveless series of appalling crimes is an ingenious plot — with a multi-million dollar prize.